Polar Bared

Kodiak Point, Book Three

Eve Langlais

Copyright © August 2014, Eve Langlais
Cover Art by Aubrey Rose © August 2014
Edited by Devin Govaere
Copy Edited by Amanda L. Pederick
Produced in Canada

Published by Eve Langlais
1606 Main Street, PO Box 151
Stittsville, Ontario, Canada, K2S1A3
http://www.EveLanglais.com

ISBN-13: 978-1501068607
ISBN-10: 1501068601

ALL RIGHTS RESERVED

Polar Bared is a work of fiction and the characters, events and dialogue found within the story are of the author's imagination and are not to be construed as real. Any resemblance to actual events or persons, either living or deceased, is completely coincidental.

No part of this book may be reproduced or shared in any form or by any means, electronic or mechanical, including but not limited to digital copying, file sharing, audio recording, email and printing without permission in writing from the author.

Prologue

"Are your men in position?" Forget hello or niceties, he asked straight out.

"Yeah. We're here, and it's fucking cold."

"I'm sure the fee is more than worth a little discomfort."

A chuckle rattled through the earpiece of his phone. "It's definitely a warm incentive. Me and the boys are already planning a hot vacation on the beach."

"Only once the task is completed. How long until you do the job?" In other words, how long until he could enact the next phase of his plan?

"Depends. We've just finished setting up camp. The boys and I will do a sweep of the surrounding area over the next few days. Get a feel for the terrain and what we can do."

"Remember, I want it to look like an accident." It was very important that no one suspect foul play.

"I know. I know. No worries. It won't be hard. Once we lure the target out to a secluded spot, we'll act."

"No one must suspect."

"Rest assured, they won't. This isn't our first hit. I'll contact you once the target is eliminated."

The line disconnected, and he stared at the disposable phone. Soon, real soon, the person plaguing him and his plans would suffer a final fate, leaving one less loose thread to worry about.

Chapter One

Run, run as fast as he could, but no matter how far and how long he fled, Boris' damning words rang through Gene's head.

"I forgive you."

The nerve of the clod-footed moose he used to call friend. As if Boris had anything to forgive. If anything, the clumsy moose should have begged Gene for forgiveness. But no. Just like everything else in his life, he didn't cooperate. Instead, Boris apologized and absolved him.

Who the fuck did that?

Gene had done bad things. *Really* bad things. He'd intentionally set out to hurt the men he once loved as brothers. He'd generated terror and pain and fear among the people living in Kodiak Point all in the name of vengeance, sweet vengeance, which wasn't exactly a warm flannel blanket on a cold winter's night, but it kept a man's spirit burning through even the darkest despair.

By all rights, Boris—good ol' cold and calculating Boris, who never hesitated to shoot when they'd faced enemy troops—should have ended Gene's life back on that impromptu battleground. Gene had intentionally baited him and trapped the moose into giving him the one-on-one fight he desired.

They'd slugged it out, the satisfying smack of his fists hitting flesh easing some of the bubbling anger inside. *At last, I will avenge myself on one of my brothers who left me to die in that cesspool overseas.*

He'd meant to kill Boris. Or he thought he did until a lovely fox named Jan pointed a gun at him and begged him to spare her lover's life. On the verge of winning, he hesitated and didn't deliver the killing blow.

What the fuck? Where inside his abused body did that shred of decency and morality come from? It bubbled past the molten lava of his betrayal and stayed his hand.

This emerging conscience made him question what was truly better. Kill Boris and live another day hating life? Or give the vixen what she wanted and, with the moose as his executioner, finally allow himself to slip into oblivion where perhaps the nightmares wouldn't follow?

What I wouldn't give for peace.

But Boris didn't finish him off. Boris showed him mercy.

Argh. Fuck. Bastard. *I hate him even more than ever.* And, at the same time, fiercely loved the goddamned prick.

Love. Hate. The emotions chased him from Kodiak Point, chased him miles and miles and miles until he took refuge in a shack he'd long ago claimed as his own.

He couldn't term it a home, but it kept the harsh elements off his clothing, bedroll, and the food he kept stashed here—most of it stolen. Apparently he'd missed the chapter in the villain's handbook that explained it was hard to hold down a job when plotting and executing revenge. So he resorted to pilfering what he needed and hunting to supplement his diet.

As he stared around at the meager surroundings, he couldn't help but think, *This is pathetic.* And little better than the prison he'd escaped. But at least he could leave anytime he wanted, no locks holding him here, and he didn't have to worry every time the door opened that death might arrive.

However, this little shack, hidden amidst the ice and snow of the Arctic Circle, wasn't exactly a safe haven. *I might still die yet.*

Several of his recent actions had placed a really large bulls-eye on his furry, white ass. Gene had done the unforgivable. He'd intentionally acted against *his* plan. It wasn't enough that Gene had walked out without a word of where he was going, no longer interested in the plot to overthrow Reid and take over the clan at Kodiak Point. Gene had actively fought against *his* army.

That would not go over well at all if the one who'd dragged him from the desert ever found out. And *he* would. *He* always did.

Gene feared few people. He could count them on one hand—the devil when he came to collect his due, his mother who would have skinned him alive for what he'd done, and *him*.

If the devil was the world's scariest demon, then *he* was his brother. An enemy like no other. Gene doubted his former army buddies had ever encountered anyone with a core of evil so great, so encompassing that it was a wonder the very foliage didn't wilt under *his* feet.

If Gene ever ran into *him* again—not intentionally that was for sure—he had no doubt he'd die. Probably painfully, unlike the merciful and quick death Boris could have given him.

Stupid, rotten jerk.

Forgiveness. As if. Just for that, Gene would return, bigger and badder than ever. Eventually. Maybe. But not right yet. First he needed some time to himself, a moment to regroup and plan.

Also known as getting wasted out of his fucking mind, sunbathing on an ice shelf and lazing around until the anger became too much again.

Or until someone literally crashed into him and forced him to face reality.

Chapter Two

Base camp resembled a mini tent city, albeit not one on a grassy plain or a sand-packed desert. Here on the northern tip of Canada's Northwest Territories, the vistas were white, white, with varying shades of white. But what could Vicky expect when she'd traveled thousands of miles to the Arctic Circle, chasing after a dream and a new start?

In the great north, civilization was but an industrial dream. The land remained virtually untouched. The air pure. There was no smog to irritate every breath or traffic noise to pollute the pristine quiet. No high-rises or roads to mar the landscape.

Majestic peaks loomed in the distance, stranded icebergs with white, snowy peaks. The fantastically curved and sometimes sheer bluffs reflected the striated glassier sheen of ice. But, apart from these, or the dark gray of the sea's edge, the only other color came from manmade sources.

Bright orange and yellow weatherproof pop-up abodes were laid out in straight lines a few hundred yards from the water. Over a dozen wind and inclement weatherproofed bubbles, each boasting an intrepid explorer. Or, in Vicky's case, a novice researcher.

Snowmobiles, and the sledges they pulled, were parked less neatly on the outskirts of this temporary town, a terrifying mode of transportation for a girl used to climate-controlled cars.

While the camp might boast a plan when it came to tents, once those temporary homes planted themselves in a spot, detritus sprang up around them. Solar panels abounded, soaking in as much of the sun's rays as possible, which wasn't much given the few hours this area got this early in spring. The batteries charged by the sun's rays would in turn power laptops and lights, as well as a myriad other small items that made tent life a little easier to bear. Which, for this city girl, was very welcome.

Vicky had never known what amenities she took for granted until she didn't have access to them or found them restricted. Hot showers? Those happened on a rotational basis with everyone in the camp, and they were timed. Get in, get clean, get dry—before you froze your butt off.

Bathroom time? Highly embarrassing for a girl who didn't even like using public washrooms. It took several days of red cheeks and clenched cheeks before she managed to get over some of her phobias.

While the interior of the tents might prove toasty, stepping outside took adjusting for a girl whose previous idea of a harsh winter included a few inches of snow on the ground and temperatures low enough to make the breath steam.

Layers and layers of cold weather gear kept the body warm, but breathing was another thing. She'd never encountered a frigidness that made a deep inhalation burn. The air was so cold up here. Cold, crisp, and fresh. Well, fresh until you entered the main living area where various cooking scents, smoke, and the general odor of people mixed together to form a unique perfume.

However, all of the rough living was worth it. Vicky was having an adventure. By herself. *With no one to tell.* But she was okay with that. Most of the time.

When she'd signed on to the expedition as a graduation present to herself, she'd held high hopes of meeting like-minded individuals and, as the brochure stated, 'forming bonds and friendships that will last a life time through an adventure shared'.

Yeah, that bond might have worked better if she was a man. While sexual harassment wasn't a problem—no one was interested in the chubby little nerd with the thick glasses—she did feel outnumbered given there was only one other female in the group of twelve.

Jackie was a nice girl, but given she'd chosen to come on this trip as a honeymoon with her new hubby, Conrad, not exactly looking to bond. Unless it was with her hubby's lips. Joined at the lips best described the pair.

Apart from Jackie, there were no other women and nobody looking to share notes and adventure with the odd one out. Everyone had their own agenda it seemed.

The guy who'd organized the expedition, while nice, was an older fellow who made it clear he was paid to be there and make sure none of the 'cidiots' hurt themselves. For the uninformed, a cidiot was a slang term used to describe a person who believed toilets were required, Wi-Fi was a must, and that coffee should be brewed over real grounds and not from instant dissolvable crystals. Sob. *I miss my Starbucks so much.*

Of the rest of the group, a few were non-English-speaking students, French by her estimation, two more in the mix were older scientists studying the climate change and its effect on the ice and water levels, and then there were the scary guys. Yeah, not exactly the nicest way to think of them, but still the first thing that popped in her head when she met them the first time.

It wasn't as if they'd done anything overt to earn that name. In reality, they looked like everyone else, they dressed the same, and, yet, something in their eyes, the set of their lips, strummed her warning meter.

It didn't help that she couldn't quite figure out what the five of them were doing here. Flinty gazed, and keeping to themselves, they went off every day to do their thing. What that thing was, she couldn't guess, and she wasn't a curious cat with a need to follow them just to find out. If she were to wager a guess, it wasn't a love of the outdoors that brought them, but other than that, what did it leave, other than illegal activities?

The company organizing the trip made them sign strict waivers about not coming along to hunt or poach, and yet, she could have sworn she'd seen one of the scary guys wearing a gun.

It could be for protection.

But in that case, why not openly wear one of the tranquilizer weapons encouraged to preserve wildlife?

Speaking of wildlife. She wasn't about to waste another day wandering aimlessly around the perimeter of camp. After several days here, she had nothing to show but pictures and more pictures of snow, ice, more snow, and, yes, more ice. How exciting.

That's not what I came for. Problem was, her goal for this trip didn't seem to coincide with anyone else's, so despite the recommendation from their guide to stick in pairs or more, Vicky had to make a decision. Play it safe and get more pictures of snow or strike out on her own? Not too far, but enough she might finally see something of interest. Something to remember when the adventure came to an end.

With some basic gear tucked into a knapsack—snacks, thermos filled with hot coffee, blanket, spare socks and thermals, flashlight, flares, and the most important item, her satellite phone—along with her camera slung around her neck for quick grabbing, Vicky set out from base camp determined to prove to herself that she could do this, cidiot gene or not.

She couldn't deny a certain trepidation. Make that a big *OhmygodIcan'tbelieveI'mdoingthis* feeling. Vicky had spent a lifetime under the thumb of others, people who told her what to do and when to do it. First her parents and then, later, her husband. Only in recent months had she begun to truly take charge of her own life. To pursue her destiny. Or at least learn to venture forth and attempt new things.

A saner person would have taken baby steps. However, Vicky decided something bolder was in order. *I need to really get out of my comfort zone.* Which was why, when she saw the ad advertising the arctic adventure, she jumped on it, not just because she wanted to do something wild but for more practical reasons too.

I need to do this for my research paper.

An older intern than most in her mid-twenties, Vicky had stumbled into the field of research and became determined to make something of herself, despite the fact her husband had mocked her choice.

"You're wasting your time," he'd say. "What will you do with the degree?"

Do? Probably nothing, but that didn't matter. She still wanted it.

Independently wealthy, her parents' untimely demise having left her with a small fortune, Vicky didn't have to work, but keeping house for two, especially when they employed a maid, meant hours of boredom. Until she discovered volunteering. Not with real people, of course, her somewhat shy nature made it hard for her to bond with others, but she'd always found it easy to relate to animals.

At the suggestion of her therapist—after many awkward sessions where she spoke quietly in one or two phrase sentences—she decided to offer her services at the local animal hospital. She enjoyed the time she spent with the animals, who she found easier to talk to than most people, even her husband.

Animals were simple to understand. They didn't care if she was nerdy or wore glasses. They didn't look at her askance if she ate that second slice of cake, although they did give her big woeful eyes in hopes of crumbs.

When the animal hospital proved too depressing, her late husband, Rick—while supportive of her volunteering was not exactly willing to let her adopt every single animal scheduled for euthanasia—suggested she volunteer for something else, which was how she ended up at the local zoo.

And where she fell in love with bears.

Not just any bears, but the polar ones.

There was something so darned adorable about them, especially the playful cubs. A *joie de vivre* seemed to inhabit the furry white beasts, and she envied it because she needed that in her life. So she volunteered to help with them. Not hands-on, of course, that was for the trained professionals, but just being around the big, cuddly creatures never failed to lift her spirits.

When new management came along, who seemed to think volunteers were a form of slave labor they could exploit, she made the hard decision to leave her beloved bears—although she visited them every weekend with her season pass to the zoo. She used her free time to go back to school.

Why not? She didn't have a job. She wasn't needed at home. In spite of Rick's mockery, Vicky decided she wanted to become a researcher. Not for money or anything. She didn't need any more. As a lawyer with a prestigious firm, Rick had made good money while alive and, when he died in the car accident, left her well off. Between his inherited assets and the lump sum the reluctant life insurance agency had to pay out, added to the money she'd come into in the last year as part of a trust her parents set up before their death, most would label her rich.

Rich, but bored.

She decided to major in zoology with a minor degree in ethology, which was the study of animals in their natural habitat. To cut a boring story short, that pending degree was why she was in the Arctic Circle, somewhere northeast of Alaska, freezing her butt off and eating lukewarm rations. Surrounded by people and yet more alone than ever.

Screw them. She didn't need her hand held while she did what she'd come out here to do. She knew how to use her GPS satellite locator. She wasn't completely inexperienced when it came to surviving outside. Of course, her previous experience, which she'd accumulated just this past summer in the woods with park rangers within screaming distance, might not have prepared her for the arctic, but she could learn. If she didn't freeze to death first.

Brrrr.

Setting off on foot, her boots sporting crampons, which were much like the golf spikes on her husband's golf shoes, she went in search of things to observe. While she was really interested in the study of polar bears, she wouldn't ignore other wildlife.

Snow geese, arctic foxes, seals, and even walruses would make welcome additions to her notes. With the age of digital cameras and virtual cloud storage, she could snap images to her heart's content. When it came to tagging and tracking specimens, she hadn't managed to score any of the prized collars with the electronic sensors to monitor the animals' every move. Those were reserved for the more intrepid researchers. Then again, that was probably for the best, as she doubted she'd actually find an animal cooperative enough to let her place one around its neck. *With my luck, if I do find an animal, it will be because I accidentally trip over it or it's hungry. Gulp.*

Considering she was wandering around on her own, it might be a good idea to not imagine the various things that could happen to her should the wildlife not prove welcoming.

In order to make her first excursion easy, she followed the sea's edge. She walked, for an hour, and didn't spot a thing. The vast white plain stretched before her, a gleaming, blinding mass with dips and swells and the occasional dangerous crevice. The dark water lapped at the edge, bereft of the movement that would have indicated life.

It was only when she stopped to take out her binoculars that she revised her plan to turn around after an hour. Thus far, the ridge she'd walked along rose as a sheer bluff from the water. But, through the far-scrying lenses, she could see in the distance a change in the vista. Slopes led down to flat shelves, frozen beaches of sorts.

I need to go there. She knew from her studies that many arctic residents preferred to hang out by sea ice. Decided, she packed away her binoculars and set off again.

And that was when things began to go wrong. As usual.

It took her about thirty minutes to reach the edge of an embankment, which sloped down instead of sheering off. A worthwhile walk because, lo and behold, she caught her first hint of life. A lonely seal pup, head bobbing in the sluggish current.

Excited, she unslung her camera and snapped a few shots. As if preening for her, the seal waddled onto shore and gave her a lovely profile to photograph. Vicky forgot the cold and discomfort as, for the first time since she'd begun this trek, she felt like a real researcher. One who needed to get closer to get the best images possible.

A quick peek around showed the dark blue water lapping at the icy ledge found at the foot of the hill. However, there was no safe or easy way down, not for a girl whose only experience climbing involved stairs when the elevator was out of service. *And I cussed and huffed the entire time.*

But survived it. What was it those buff trainers at the gym told her, no pain, no gain? She could do this.

"You stay right there, Mr. Seal," she muttered. "I'm not done with you yet."

Determined to locate an easier angle of descent, she decided to go a little farther, but only after a long pull from her Thermos of the barely warm stuff that called itself coffee, bitter tasting even with the loads of sugar dumped in it.

Perhaps it was the hot shining sun, or the fact that, as she went to tuck her coffee canister away, she fumbled her knapsack and dropped it. Whatever the reason, as she bent to grab her bag, a wave of dizziness struck. Whoa.

Lightheaded, she blinked a few times and shook her head. It didn't do much to dispel the odd lethargy invading her body. How odd. She took a step and wobbled on her feet. Another step and she slid on a patch of ice—cleats or not.

She windmilled her arms in an attempt to regain her balance and failed. With an oomph, she landed on her bum, and that should have been the end of it, except she landed hard enough to cause a chunk of ice and snow to crack off from the edge she stood on.

Uh-oh.

Before she could yell, off she went. On her makeshift sled, she tobogganed, down the sloped embankment, which might have been fun in other circumstances, but as she eyed the killer cold water lapping at the edge of the ice, which she skidded toward with no means of slowing down or stopping? Yeah. Not a good scenario. She would have screamed if the cold air she sucked in didn't have her choking.

Throwing herself to her side did nothing, and neither did flipping to her tummy, other than throw snow into her face and fogging her glasses so she could only perceive her imminent demise in blurry snatches. She tried to slow her rapid flight, digging for purchase on smooth ice with her gloved fingers.

Ha, that did nothing to reduce her speed, but the wild flailing did somewhat veer her trajectory, aiming her toward a white, snowy hump, which if she was lucky—*Please please please*—would jolt her to a stop or, if her clumsiness prevailed, would launch her rocketing body and send her plunging to an icy-cold death.

Curse you, vivid imagination!

Unable to watch, she closed her eyes just before impact. She hit the furry mound, and the breath was knocked out of her, but, good news, she stopped. She panted, hair-like strands sticking to her lips and getting inhaled with each breath.

Wait a second. Furry mound?

Face buried in what was most definitely hair, she stopped breathing. Only one animal with this kind of mass had thick fur of snow white. She would have gulped if she wasn't so terrified.

When she'd come on her expedition to study polar bears in their natural habitat, she'd meant to do so from afar, where it was safe. Or approaching after nailing it with a few tranquilizer darts to ensure it was sleeping soundly.

With her backpack who knew where, the putting-it-to-sleep option was out. She could think of no Plan B.

But maybe she panicked for nothing. Perhaps this bear was dead. After all she'd hit it pretty hard, and it hadn't budged. *Could be the bear is sleeping deeply and won't wake up? Maybe—*

Massive muscles shifted against her buried face as the mound moved, and she craned her head to peek, morbid curiosity not allowing her to stay hidden. Even through her blurry lenses—her glasses miraculously still on her face—she noted the bright blue eyes glaring at her and the lips on a muzzle pulled back in a vicious snarl.

Wow, what big teeth it has.

It growled.

She fainted.

Chapter Three

Nothing like napping in the sun.

Much like a lazy pussy, Gene basked in the warm rays that would last only a few hours this early in spring.

A part of Gene knew he should move or maybe at least take a sniff around and make sure where he'd passed out the night before was safe. And he meant passed out, as in snookered-out-of-his-mind wasted. Last thing he recalled was collapsing flat on his belly with no real thought other than, 'Hey, this piece of ice is comfy'.

Now, you might wonder, how did a big ol' fucking polar bear get his paws on some booze somewhere in the Arctic Circle far from annoying reminders of his past? Simple. This time of the year saw plenty of explorers pitching a tent in the hopes of bragging rights.

He gave them something to brag about, although, he doubted many included the part where they pissed their pants when he sliced open the side of their tent, stuck his head in, and roared. While they scurried off screaming, he nosed around, not really interested in their food—icky freeze-dried rations—but they often had the one thing he did want. Pepper.

While he did so love a yummy fresh seal, he preferred it with a dash of the peppery stuff. Too lazy to head to his hidey-hole and his stash of goods, in case he had some company he preferred to avoid, he currently found it easier to raid campers for supplies. The bottle of booze he'd scored, a full gallon of ridiculously potent moonshine, was a bonus, one that didn't last the night.

While his kind might metabolize alcohol faster than humans, drink enough of it in a short time frame and they could get as smashed as the next guy. And Gene needed to get smashed. Zonkered. Anything to forget the fucking assholes back in Kodiak Point.

Well over a month, or was it two, since his match with the moose and he still hadn't formed a proper plan. Still hadn't mustered enough rage to go after the others he hated so much. Still didn't know what he wanted to do. Other than eat, sleep, and terrify the occasional idiot in a tent.

Oh and avoid his shack because of concerns it was compromised. He had no real reason to think so other than a gut instinct, one that said don't get complacent in one spot or he might just end up as a rug.

Something that might happen anyway given he found himself sunning who the fuck knew where and was too lazy to figure it out. He made a tempting target for hunters, but given this area wasn't known for illegal poaching, it being a research hot spot for every Tom, Dick, and Harry with a camera and a web cam, he felt pretty safe.

Until something plowed into him.
What the fuck?

It better not be those pesky snow geese again. Feathers or not, I will eat them if they're doing it on purpose to piss me off. Bird-brained little idiots.

Rousing his shaggy head, he craned to peer at the—sniff—human female who'd skidded into his side. *Where the hell did she come from?*

She raised her head timidly and blinked at him through skewed and misted glasses. Then she face planted.

Lily-livered women! Whether he encountered them as a beast or a man, they just couldn't handle the sight of him.

He snorted as he stretched his muscles, her surprise arrival putting an end to his siesta. Where there was one human, there were usually more. Usually. Oddly enough though, he didn't hear or scent any. *Don't tell me this idiot is roaming alone?*

On four paws, he rose, a hefty ton and a bit of predator with white fur, sharp claws, and a rumbling belly.

Smells good. That remark came from his bear. But Gene agreed. Whoever she was, she did and not just in a red-meat kind of way. He let himself nose the hair peeking from underneath her wooly hat. Honey-scented shampoo. *Yum.* It wasn't just brown and black bears who liked sweet things. Gene possessed a sweet tooth too. And this woman smelled *good*.

Good enough to eat, and he didn't mean as food. While his polar dick didn't rise for the girl, mentally, his human side couldn't deny a certain ardent interest.

Attraction? Fuck, how long since that emotion had plagued him? Even odder, it was for a human woman he'd only gotten a glimpse of, a second really, where he got only an impression of big brown eyes and a pink mouth rounded in an O of surprise. A mouth perfectly shaped for—

He shook his head. *Keep your mind on the situation, soldier.* He could practically hear his old sergeant's bark. *Who is she, and what is she doing out here?*

Or the better question, why was she alone? Surely by now someone would have come running to the edge of the slope or called out to see if she was all right?

Other than the lap of water against ice, nothing echoed, either near or far.

Strange. But not as strange as her arrival. Who was she? Curiosity made him want to see the woman who'd more or less landed in his lap.

With a paw, he carefully flipped her over onto her back, sparing her face from the frostbite she'd surely get if she remained plastered to the cold surface he'd chosen to nap on.

Tan skin, rounded cheeks, pert nose, and dark hair wisping out from the edges of her cap. Latina or Italian descent he'd wager. Dark-rimmed glasses sat crookedly on her face, and he could have tsked the fact she'd forgotten to wear protective goggles.

Amateur.

He eyed the rest of her, pegging her at about five foot and a few inches, chubby perhaps or really well layered in winter clothing. Given the name brands she wore, he doubted it. That kind of quality didn't rely on bulk to keep its wearer warm.

Around her neck she wore a camera, while a few yards away sat a backpack. Great. Another bloody gawker.

What was it with people who felt a need to travel to the Great White North and take pictures? If you wanted to see what a polar bear looked like, do an Internet search or, better yet, visit a local zoo.

Just leave him, his misery, and his sea ice the fuck alone.

Wake up on the wrong side of the ice pack? Damned straight he did and had for the last several years.

She stirred with a soft sigh, and he backed away. Just because she looked harmless didn't mean she didn't have a gun stashed in a pocket or a tranquilizer hidden in her glove. Jan, foxy secretary to the asshole Reid, was a prime example of don't trust outward appearances. The vixen looked so prim and proper on the outside, but Jan could shoot to kill and not bat a lash.

Gene could almost envy Boris his luck in snaring Jan as his mate. Almost. If it didn't mean having to tolerate another person at his side for the rest of his life.

No way. Gene wasn't interested in getting hitched. Damned women with their weeping and wailing and drama. He preferred the single life. It was quieter. Less cluttered. Besides, it wasn't as if any woman would ever want him.

Scarred soldiers suffering from PTSD who went furry and liked hurting things weren't considered prime husband material.

Hell, with his perpetual scowl, sometimes even getting laid was a chore.

But that didn't always used to be the case.

He slammed that door to his past shut before it could creep open.

No point in looking in there. The boy he used to be had died a long time ago. There was no going back for him. Not after all he'd suffered and done.

With one last look at the woman—a look with more longing than he expected—he turned his back and lumbered off, the refreshing sea calling his name. He ignored his conscience, which said he should stick around and ensure her safety. He ignored the little voice that said he should at least find out her name. Why bother?

Bad guys don't get the girl.

Chapter Four

Bright sunlight burned against her eyelids, and yet a deep cold radiated at Vicky's back.

Where am I? Last thing she remembered—
Bear!

Nothing like extreme fear to get the blood pumping. Vicky scrambled to her feet and spun around in a circle looking for the massive polar bear she'd used as a cushion for her landing. It was gone, and yay for her, she was still here with all her body parts intact.

I'm alive!

Finally luck was shining on her, although, she would have preferred her luck to include a few pictures of the bear. Studying the wildlife was what she'd come out here for. Wouldn't it figure that her first really awesome find and she fainted, an annoying habit of hers when her stress levels got too high? It used to drive her father, and then Rick, nuts.

Yell at her too much or raise a heavy fist, and boom, she hit the ground. Her body's self-defense mechanism. Finding the courage to go on an adventure hadn't wiped out her knack. Good thing because her ignoble face plant probably saved her from becoming lunch.

Peeking around, she couldn't spot either the polar bear or the seal she'd originally set out to investigate. Double bummer. With the fright wearing off, she really wished she could have snapped some pics so she could have something to show for her excursion.

A slight blur of motion caught her eye. Squinting in the glare from the sun hitting ice and snow, she studied the bobbing ice floe a few yards from shore, where she thought she'd spotted something. There it was again. A twitch of something moving. Grabbing her camera, she zoomed in on the spot and was rewarded.

It's my polar bear. The one that stopped her mad slide, the one that didn't eat her, the one that stared right back at her. Gulp.

Eyeing him with her zoom lens, she held her breath, waiting to see if he'd dive in the cold waves and return for a visit. When he didn't seem inclined to leave his cold island and maul her for a meal, she took advantage, snapping pictures of him.

He was a big fellow, and a survivor. One just had to see the jagged scar bisecting his face to know he'd fought to stay alive. It made her wonder what he'd encountered that was tough enough to hurt him so bad. Something almost as tough as a polar bear?

Eep. I wouldn't want to run into that. Her deep shudder acted as a reminder she should head back to base camp. Spring might mean longer daylight hours, but she didn't want to get caught out here once darkness fell. Not only was she not equipped for it, having left her tent and sleeping bag behind in favor of traveling light, but she'd seen enough horror movies to know that roaming around after dark, in the arctic, was a sure way to get eaten by ancient ice monsters who craved warm-blooded meat.

Shiver.

Shoving her glasses to force them back onto the bridge of her nose, she sighed. They slanted drunkenly.

Bent. Again. She yanked the lenses off and studied them. Nose piece or arm? Having worn glasses for as long as she could remember—contact lenses proving annoying to someone who couldn't aim a finger at her eyeball without clamping it shut— she had plenty of experience righting crooked parts.

And snapping them.

The needed straightening of the left arm on her frames resulted in them separating. Not unexpected given how many times she'd fixed them at this point, but certainly inconvenient given her spare pairs were back in her tent. While she could see through the glasses if she held her head at a certain angle, they certainly wouldn't survive the climbing it appeared she'd have to do.

Better save them for when I need them. Before she tucked them into her pocket, she took stock of her situation and location. She currently found herself on a rather flat shelf at the bottom of the icy slope she'd tobogganed down. A steep slope, she might add. The shelf itself extended probably a hundred yards or so along the sea's edge, and the sharply angled hill followed it. Which was bad. Real bad.

She walked the length of the icy beach, looking for a part of it where the incline wasn't so steep. In some spots it was almost perfectly vertical. In others, it sloped, like the spot she'd careened down. Problem was getting back up it.

When she realized she wouldn't find an easy path off the ledge or, even better, a set of stairs, she resigned herself to the fact she'd have to climb.

Sigh. She hated climbing. Chubby girls weren't meant to yank their body weight up inclines where gravity seemed determined to work against them. But she tried.

Glasses stowed away safely in a pocket—what was left of them—and backpack firmly attached to her, she took a deep breath in front of the spot with the best angle of ascent.

I can do this.

Leaning her weight forward and using her hands and feet, she tried to clamber up the icy surface.

She made it about a third of the way up—okay, so it was more like a quarter—before she lost her footing and went sliding backwards.

"Eeek!" She couldn't help the scream as she skidded, fearful of a polar plunge. Luckily, her momentum didn't bring her to the edge, but it did scare the hell out of her.

On her next attempt, she didn't make it as far. The one after that even less. With each try she got more tired, more frustrated and by the fourth failure, she couldn't help the tears in her eyes, which partially had to do with the fact she'd whacked her face against the ice pack when she slipped.

This isn't working.

Morose at her lack of agility, and wishing she'd thought to pack some ice picks, she plopped herself in a seated position at the bottom and glared at the hill that mocked her. She took more sips of her sludge-like coffee, hoping for a caffeine boost but, instead, feeling more and more tired. Her spirits dragged her down.

Much as it galled her, she'd have to admit defeat and call for help. All adventurers were given the excursion leader's contact number. When she'd programmed it into her phone, she'd never expected to have to use it. *I can just imagine how the camp will mock me. Geek girl goes on simple walk and requires saving.* Talk about handing people fodder to ridicule her.

But she could handle the teasing and name-calling. It wouldn't be the first time in her life she had to put up with it. Even Rick, rest his soul, had subjected her to snide remarks. *Hey, honey, are you sure you should stay out in the sun so long? I think I smell bacon cooking.* Sometimes he could be a bit of an insensitive jerk. However, now was not the time to think ill of the dead.

It took a few minutes of digging around in her pack, but Vicky located her satellite phone. State-of-the-art, guaranteed to work in even the toughest conditions—or so the salesman assured her. She'd tested it out a few times before the trip. In populated areas.

Out here in the arctic? Yeah, it didn't quite work as advertised.

"Satellite, my butt," she muttered, looking at the no-service box that popped up on the screen. She held it up in the air. No change. She walked to one end of the shelf then the other, holding it aloft, shaking it, cursing it, and at one point, throwing it at the cliff face. Cursing again as she scrabbled after it on her hands and knees, one hand holding her glasses in place as she searched for it among the cracks and bumps it landed among.

No matter what she did, the damned thing wouldn't give her a single bar. Not one.

"Is it so much to ask that something goes right in my life?" she yelled to the sky. "Just for once, could I have some good luck?"

She couldn't help it. She sat down and sniffled, the cold seeping into her bones, the dreaded fatigue making her droop.

Already at her lowest, Karma, with her sadistic sense of humor, answered her rant in the form of a big, probably hungry polar bear that emerged from the sea waters, water sluicing from its fur. In shock, her jaw dropped, her throat locked and Vicky stared unblinking as it lumbered in her direction.

Forget remembering to take a picture. For the second time that day, Vicky's face got acquainted with the ice.

Chapter Five

What am I doing here?

Gene meant to leave the girl behind. He truly did because that was how bad guys acted. It was in the villain handbook somewhere. *Don't give a shit about anyone, especially strangers. Even cute ones.*

He knew that. His bear knew that, and yet for some inexplicable reason, he'd no sooner left the woman than he circled around. Paddling to an ice floe with a hump, he clambered aboard and inched his way along it until he could spy on the beach he'd left behind, and its occupant.

A silent spectator, he observed as she roused from her faint and took stock of her surroundings. His hiding spot wasn't the best, his bulk larger than the swell on his floating berth. She caught a glimpse of him and took pictures. Lots of them.

Ack. Gene hated technology, and he especially hated having his photo taken, but that still didn't send him on his merry way.

Nope. He perched there on his floating isle and kept an eye on her. It proved more entertaining than expected. He noted her dilemma in escaping and then chuffed in inescapable amusement as her various attempts to climb met with failure. He'd never seen a more pathetic and head-shaking, disbelieving moment as her slipping and sliding over and over down the hill. Did the girl not have any basic ice-climbing equipment? Apparently not because she stopped after several failures. When he saw her dig out a phone, he almost left.

At least she could call for help. Probably the first smart thing he'd seen her do since he'd encountered her. Except, judging by her dancing and prancing, and the flinging of said phone, she seemed to be experiencing signal issues. Not uncommon depending on her carrier.

Worldwide coverage to a phone provider meant worldwide cities, not icy plateaus in the arctic. A fact the woman was realizing—and sniffling over.

Such a useless reaction. Crying wouldn't solve her problem. Sitting on her butt wouldn't either. Then again, what else could she do? At this point she needed a hero to rescue her.

Sigh.

I'm not a fucking hero.

But he also couldn't just let her sit there. Why, he couldn't have said. He totally admitted he was a dick. The first to volunteer if someone needed violence accomplished or mayhem to explode. And totally into the whole vengeance gig.

Rescuing stupid women who went off on their own, ill equipped, not prepared and unlucky beyond belief? Someone else's job.

What if there is no someone else? How long before someone noticed she'd gone missing? Before a search party was sent out?

Could she survive the coming cold of night? Fend off any possible wild animals? Because Gene wasn't the only thing with teeth and claws that roamed the frozen plains.

Another big sigh.

I don't fucking believe I'm about to do this. Into the frigid water he slid, which he didn't mind given his polar bear packed an insulating layer that kept him from freezing to death.

Paddling over to the sea shelf, he couldn't help but note when she realized he approached. Her eyes grew wide behind her crooked glasses, and she keeled over.

She fainted. Again. Did the girl not have a courageous bone in her body? He knew not all women were so weak-hearted.

From what he'd heard through the rumor mill, Reid's human mate, Tammy, had taken on his Kodiak bear form armed with only a frying pan. As for poised and blonde Jan? She never went anywhere unarmed. Gene's less-than-intrepid researcher? She took a nap.

She so doesn't belong out here. Especially not alone.

As Gene emerged from the sea, he shook himself, sending droplets of water flying. He couldn't help but think that at least if she remained unconscious she'd probably make his annoying rescue of her much easier. Hysterical women grated on his nerves.

But speaking of rescue, exactly how would he get her up the hill? In his bear form, he couldn't exactly carry her, and yet, in his human form, which would entail nudity in freezing temperatures—which he could handle for a little while before suffering—he would have the same problem she did in clambering up the incline.

He would need the traction his paws and claws could give him, which meant dragging her.

Fuck I hope no one is around to tape this. He could just imagine the YouTube sensation.

Polar Bear drags unconscious woman off to its lair.

He preferred headlines more along the lines of *Polar bear eats idiot who thought he could videotape him and post the fucking thing online.*

It soon became apparent that dragging her uphill was going to have more challenges than expected. Such as how to do it without trampling her. She was a tad larger than a fish. A lot more fragile than a seal. And since the whole purpose behind his act was to keep her alive, bouncing her head off the ice might not prove the best recourse.

With a growl, he shifted shapes and stood, hands on his hips, glaring down at her.

"What am I going to do with you?" he muttered aloud.

She would, of course, take that moment to flutter her eyes open, blink, take in his appearance, and then, instead of screaming as expected, replied, in a slurred voice, "Wow. Can I suggest you do me?"

Well, that was unexpected. He surely misunderstood. "What the fuck did you say?"

She squinted, her glasses lost or tucked away. "You are naked."

"Very."

"Why?"

"Why what?"

"Why are you naked? It's cold out here." As if to make that point clear, she shivered. "So cold."

He held in yet another sigh. "You need to get somewhere warm before you die."

"You mean I'm not dead yet?"

"Emphasis on the yet," he grumbled.

"Oh. I guess I'm close then. That would explain why I'm hallucinating a giant naked man is talking to me."

She thought him a hallucination? That might actually work in his favor.

"This is all a dream."

A sigh escaped her. "Figures. I never have good ones. Why can't I have one where I'm on a warm beach? With you naked still of course." She smiled and giggled.

Gene frowned. Someone was feeling the effects of being out in the cold for too long. It happened. Something about the air, and other mumbo jumbo shit he didn't pay much attention to. As a shifter he didn't suffer from normal human frailties.

But she apparently did.

"Do you have a name?" he asked as he bent down to pick her up.

"Victoria, but people usually call me Vicky. Or Trippy. I'm a little clumsy," she said in an almost whisper, as if confiding in him.

Clumsy was understating it from what he'd seen so far. With her in his arms, he faced the dilemma of how to climb the hill. He solved it the same way he had in the desert with one of his fallen mates. "I'm going to put you on my back. I need you to hold tight around my neck and wrap your legs around my waist."

"You want me to piggyback you?"

"Yes," he said, shifting her around his torso.

She clung to him, her chin resting on his shoulder, her limbs snug around him. It warmed him more than it should have.

"Don't let go,' he warned as he began to climb.

"I won't. I can do anything in a dream," she announced. "I can pretend I'm skinny and beautiful. I can meet strange naked men. I can even kiss them."

And she did. She planted a sloppy smooch on his neck, and he almost lost his footing.

"What the hell was that for?" he barked.

"A thank you?" she said in a meek voice.

"You don't need to thank me. This is a dream, remember?" He practically growled the words at her but couldn't erase the sizzling heat of her embrace. When was the last time a woman kissed him without him getting her drunk first?

Then again, given Vicky's loopy state, she wasn't far off. Someone carried around some good shit in her canteen. *Which makes her an even bigger idiot than I thought.*

She sighed, her breath a warm flutter on the skin of his neck. "I know it's a dream. As if a handsome guy would actually come to my rescue. Things like that don't happen to me."

Such defeatist words. For some reason he didn't care for them. "Then they're idiots."

"I wish. But I can't blame them. I'm not exactly the type to inspire grand gestures. Short, chubby geeks with glasses don't inspire passion."

He begged to differ. Cold outside or not, she had the most stimulating effect on a certain body part. "I don't know what you're talking about. I think you're fine the way you are."

She snorted. "God, if only you were real instead of a figment of my imagination."

They reached the top of the slope with the soles of his feet burning from the cold, his fingers bruised and torn from the icy climb, but at least he'd gotten her out of danger. Or had he?

Her teeth had stopped chattering, and her next words emerged slurred, and sleepy. "Thanks, handsome naked guy, for saving me, but now if you don't mind, I think I'll have a nap." The grip around his neck slackened, as did the legs around his waist, and she began to slide off his body.

"Don't you dare," he growled. "I did not just carry you up that fucking hill so you could pass out from the cold now. Get on your feet, woman!"

He might have said it in his most commanding tone, but Vicky proved too groggy to listen. Unnaturally so. But Gene didn't have time to ponder it. He needed to get her somewhere safe. Twilight approached quickly, along with colder temperatures.

He had no idea where her camp was. Not a clue if anyone was seeking her out. And for some reason, he was plagued with an inability to ditch her or wring her neck to quickly put her out of her misery—and solve his problem.

"Fuck me to hell and back," a place he'd visited during the war and never intended to return. Why couldn't he just leave her there? She wasn't his responsibility. She meant nothing to him.

Yet, that didn't stop him from swapping forms, and by holding the hood of her parka to keep her head from bumping on the ground, he part dragged her then carried her until the cold got too much before dragging her again until he reached the place he called home, which luckily for them both wasn't too far from where he'd passed out the night before.

More good news? There wasn't anybody waiting for him. No one took a shot. And all his shit was intact. The bad news? The inside wasn't much warmer than the outside.

Depositing Vicky on the cot he kept, he went over to the qulliq in the corner of his hut. An Inuit version of a stove and lamp, the qulliq was made of carved soapstone, it resembled a basin. From a box he kept outside, he grabbed some chunks of frozen seal oil and put it in the hollow of his qulliq and lit it. It smoked a bit, but it couldn't be helped. He'd run out of Beluga blubber, which was the best fuel, burning hot and practically smokeless.

A fire lit, though, didn't mean an immediately warm home. Vicky lay still on his cot, past the point of shivering, her skin pale, too pale and cold.

There was no getting around it. If he wanted to warm her up, he'd have to resort to old-fashioned methods. Good thing he hadn't gotten dressed yet.

Chapter Six

What a strange dream.

One moment, Vicky was on the icy ledge, certain she'd freeze to death, and the next, a giant polar bear appeared, the same as before she was certain given she doubted many of them shared the same distinctive bisecting scar down its face.

For the second time that day, she fainted. Forget adversity turning her into some super-duper woman capable of incredible adrenalized feats. She didn't have time for conscious thought, although if she had, it might have veered along the lines of, *Oh my god, he's coming back to eat me.* She hit the ice faster than she could blink.

Turned out she would have been totally wrong about the whole eating thing. Nope, instead, according to her foggy recollection, things got weird. Dazed and confused, she vaguely seemed to remember the bear attempting to drag her up the hill. Which made no sense. If it was going to eat her, why not tear into her while she lay practically comatose?

But no. Bouncing her off the humps and bumps, the polar bear tried to haul her upward. It didn't work. The darned hill just wouldn't cooperate.

The bear gave up. And this was where the real hallucination began. Suddenly, the bear was gone, and a naked man took its place. As naked men went, holy smokes!

Even with no glasses, she had no problem seeing the guy was built like some kind of body builder. Or wrestler. His muscles had muscles, and she got to touch them. Kind of.

First, her imaginary naked hero attempted to pick her up princess style, which was utterly cool. She'd never had a guy do that before, dream or not. However, that didn't last because he also couldn't maneuver the blasted slippery slope.

Kudos to him, he didn't give up. Her chivalrous naked knight had her piggyback him. Even for a dream, the whole string of events was odd, but oddest of all was the desire she had to straddle his front and not his back. Such a naughty thing for her to think. Brazen too, as brazen as what she did next.

I can't believe dream-me had the nerve to give him a kiss. On the cheek, but still, that was bold by her standards.

Her dead husband wasn't one to enjoy emotional displays. They rarely did more than peck, and when he did his husbandly duty, in the dark, every few weeks, there was little touching of any body parts. But it had always been that way since they first started dating when she was seventeen until his death six years later.

Really, she had to wonder what the big deal was about sex. Sure, she didn't have much experience to measure by—she had, after all, married her high school sweetheart and hadn't dated since his demise—but still, she couldn't imagine the big fuss. It was okay.

Except, kissing her dream rescuer wasn't the same. It was hot. Just not hot enough to stop the cold from making her fall asleep and missing what happened next. What a dull ending to a hot dream.

Or was that the end?

Because for one thing, she wasn't dead. Nor was she cold any longer. On the contrary, every inch of her was toasty warm pressed as it was against a very naked, male body.

Naked?

Male body?

Eek!

Her eyes popped open, but she didn't see much given her face was smooshed against some smooth skin and a blanket seemed to cover her head. The biggest question though was, whose skin did she cuddle?

Barely daring to breath, she listened and took stock of what she could perceive. Visually, nothing, but physically… Damn, the bare chest she rested against wasn't the only thing lacking clothing.

I'm naked too. Naked and cocooned in a set of arms that wrapped around her with ease and thick legs that trapped her own. Oh, and whoever did the hugging really seemed to enjoy the pose, or so the jab against her stomach indicated.

Oh this is bad. So very, very bad.

While she'd lain unconscious dreaming of polar bears and a muscled, naked man, someone, a stranger, had found her and taken her back to his lair and stripped her to…

Cuddle? Or had more nefarious things taken place while she was unconscious?

"I know you're awake," a deep voice declared, the rumble of it vibrating against her cheek where it lay his chest.

"No, I'm not." Oops, had she said that aloud?

Judging by his heavy sigh? She had.

"Yes, you are. Finally. Or are you going to faint again just to prove me wrong?"

She winced. He'd seen her doing that, had he? "I'll try not to pass out again. But I can't help it. It happens when I get really scared."

"Then we might have a problem."

"Why, do you intend to frighten me?" Again, she spoke without thinking then cringed. What was wrong with her? She was in an unknown place plastered to a naked man, and here she was trying to intentionally goad him.

"Not on purpose. However, I can't help my looks."

He thought she'd faint because he was butt ugly? She wasn't that shallow. Actually, she liked to think she wasn't shallow at all, just timid. "I'm more frightened right now because of…um…that is…" She couldn't state that the fact they were glued together skin to skin was the scariest thing right now. What did he intend? What had he already done? What did he want with her?

A thread of amusement entered his reply. "In case you're wondering, we're naked in this sleeping bag together because it's the best and fastest way to warm someone suffering from hypothermia. So don't freak out. Keeping you alive is the only reason we're plastered together."

"Oh." Of course he'd have a rational explanation. So why was she a tad disappointed her unknown rescuer didn't feel a need to ravish her?

"I did not take advantage of the situation." She let out a sigh of relief. "But I could have," he added more ominously.

She squeaked and went still, holding even her breath.

"Did you faint?" he asked in that deep rumble of his that slid over her skin in a most intriguing fashion.

"No." Was that her sounding defensive?

"It's a miracle," was his sarcastic reply.

Smartass. She wisely kept that retort to herself. "So how long do we need to stay like this?" she asked, not that she was in any hurry to move. Truly, if he meant her no harm, then their current situation could be counted as pleasant. Perhaps even more than pleasant. The more she took stock of the situation, and enjoyed the sensation of a very muscular body pressed against her, the more her body heated and butterflies fluttered in her lower belly.

"Are you warm?" he asked.

More than she'd been since she'd come to the arctic. She nodded, her cheek rubbing against the smooth skin of his chest.

He made a sound. "In that case then, I'm going to slip out of this sleeping bag and put on some clothes."

Light penetrated the dark cocoon as the hood of fabric he'd drawn over her was pulled back. His furnace-like heat evaporated, and she almost called him back.

Which was nuts. Why on earth would she want a complete stranger to crawl back in bed with her?

Probably because he had the nicest butt she'd ever seen. Actually, all of him was pretty darned hot. Even without her glasses, Vicky could see his tight glutes, his corded thighs, his muscled back. When she squinted, she also noted the scars.

"What happened to you?"

Without turning, he pulled a shirt over his head and answered with a gruff, "None of your fucking business."

Not the talkative type. She clamped her mouth shut. Clothes came flying her way, hitting her in the face when she wasn't quick enough to get her hands raised in time.

"Get dressed."

With those brusque words, he left the hut, taking time only to shove his feet in boots without lacing them and grabbing a jacket, all without showing her his face. As she dressed, with blurry eyes, she peered around.

While not in a tent, the shack, which wasn't any larger, didn't boast much. It contained the cot she'd cuddled in with her mysterious rescuer, some kind of weird burning basin in a corner, and boxes from which peeked food items and gear. She noted no personal effects, nothing to tell her anything of the man who never said where he'd gone or if he'd come back.

No matter, at least she was warm, there was food, and she was alive. Better than she could have expected given her ignoble face plant in front of the polar bear. At least now she had an explanation for her strange dream of rescue by a naked man.

The stranger must have saved her from the bear and carried her back here, dressed of course because only a mad man would brave the elements without a stitch of clothing.

She must have awoken briefly, long enough to catch a glimpse of his nudity before he snuggled her, and her muddled subconscious took care of the rest, sending her a wild dream. *My very first erotic dream.* And hopefully not her last.

Mouth pasty, she swung her legs out of the bed and stood. Surely he had some water around here somewhere? However, short of crouching to glance in every box, she couldn't tell, and she didn't want to snoop.

She did spot her bag, though, by the door. The thermos of coffee, surely cold by now, still had some liquid. Not the most palatable thing, but at least it would moisten her palate so her tongue didn't stick.

Unscrewing the lid, she'd just poured a cup when he re-entered.

"What are you doing?" he barked. She barely had a moment to lift her head and look at him before he'd knocked the insulated cup from her hand, sending the liquid splashing.

"You spilled my coffee," she said, stating the obvious.

"Because I wanted you to stay awake. Can you not smell the chemicals in it? Of course you can't," he said, replying to his own odd query. "Give me a minute and I'll make some fresh, untainted coffee."

As he pulled a battered coffee pot from a shelf overhead and poured grinds into the top— real coffee grinds!—she found herself asking, to his back, since he'd turned abruptly from her once again before giving her more than just a bare glimpse of his face, "What did you mean when you said you smelled chemicals? I realize it's instant coffee, but the FDA says everything in it is safe."

"Safe yes, but it's the sleeping agent it's laced with that I'd prefer you stay away from. Or were you planning to snore the day away again?"

Her coffee was laced with a drug? But why? And by who? And more interestingly, how the heck could he smell it?

She didn't voice any of those queries, instead sticking to the most important one in her mind considering her current situation. "Who are you?"

"Nobody."

"Hi, Nobody, my name is Vicky." Where she found the gumption to tease she would never know. Perhaps it was the lingering effect of the supposed drug in her java. It did, however, finally get him to turn her way.

The flickering glow of the fire lit his face while giving it deep shadows, but even without her glasses, she could tell he was handsome in a craggy, hard-lined kind of way. Square chin, bristled jaw, slightly crooked nose, piercing blue eyes, shocking white brush-cut hair. All in all, a strong face. A tough face. One with a scar that went from his forehead down to his mouth. Ouch.

"Take a picture, it will last longer," he snarled.

"I'm sorry." She dropped her gaze.

"I warned you I was scary."

A frown creased her brow, and she dared to raise her eyes for a second. "It's not your face that frightens me, but your bark." Heat rushed to her cheeks at her accusation, and she quickly stared at her hands again, waiting for his rebuke or, as Rick occasionally did when stressed or a little drunk, a cuff for speaking out of line.

"I don't bark," was his rebuttal.

"If you say so." What was it with her today?

"I do. Here's your coffee." He thrust a dented metal cup into her hands, and she cradled it as she sat back on the edge of the bed.

"Are you hungry?"

She nodded.

"Oatmeal okay?"

Another nod. It seemed safest given his volatile mood. Hadn't she learned from her marriage to Rick to not push men when they were on the edge? Had she so quickly forgotten the lessons they'd taught her, Rick and her father?

Her father, God rest his soul, had certain beliefs when it came to a woman's role in life, beliefs he firmly enforced. Stepping out of line resulted in rebukes, mostly verbal ones, but the occasional slap wasn't unheard of. When her parents died and Rick took charge, the disciplining trend continued. Not because she wanted it to, but what else could she do? Rick was her husband, and while she was smart enough to realize his treatment of her wasn't completely right, she didn't know how to stop it.

Then he died.

And I came to life. Or at least was trying to live life differently than before, with more bravery. It seemed, though, that her past habits still lurked.

A bowl entered her line of sight, and she set her mug down to grasp it. Quietly, she dipped her spoon in and ate.

The silence stretched, and stifled.

He broke it first. "Why aren't you chattering away like women always do?"

Should she lie and say she was tired? Or should she try to live by her new motto of be brave? "I don't want to make you angry."

He growled. "I will get angry if you flinch one more time when I talk to you. I'm not going to hurt you."

Funny, because he sure sounded like he might, especially now that she'd told him her real reason for silence. Frightened, she kept her head ducked and didn't reply.

Once again, silence reigned. He sighed. "Where's your camp?"

She shrugged and meekly replied, "I don't know."

"Is it along the sea shelf where I found you?"

"I know we're by the water. I have the coordinates on my phone."

"Who are you staying with? Why were you alone when I found you? What are you doing out here?"

He tossed questions out at her rapidly, and she did her best to answer.

"I'm with an expedition. We're here for a month to take in the scenery and experience living in the arctic. I was alone because no one in the group wanted to come with me." Or so she assumed. She'd never technically asked anyone, too shy to butt her way into a group.

"How did your coffee end up drugged?"

His last question saw her finally raising her gaze. He snared and held it. What blue eyes he had. Beautiful eyes with dark lashes. "No one drugged it. I made it myself."

"Were you trying to commit suicide?"

"What?" Her eyes widened. "Of course not."

"Then, I'll ask again, why was your coffee drugged?"

"I don't know, but it wasn't me. And why are you so convinced it was?" Since he seemed to want to open a dialogue, she felt safe in answering. For now.

"Reason number one, I could smell the chemicals."

"How?"

"Think of it as a finely tuned sense of smell."

Perhaps the lack of air pollutants was the reason for his olfactory ability. "What's the other reason?

"You were kind of out of it yesterday when I found you on that ice shelf. Almost like you were drunk."

It just occurred to Vicky she'd forgotten something very important. "Thank you by the way for saving me. If not for you, I would have gotten eaten by the bear or frozen to death."

He grunted. "Whatever."

"How did you scare off the bear? You didn't kill it, did you?"

Even without her glasses, she could see the corner of his lip curl in amusement. "No, the bear is very much alive."

She sighed in relief.

"It matters to you?"

"Of course. It wasn't the bear's fault I stumbled on to him. I'd hate to see such a beautiful creature killed for being where he belonged doing what comes naturally."

"And you think eating pesky women is natural?"

Again, her cheeks heated. "I don't mean to be a bother. Just point me in the direction you found me, and I'll leave you alone."

"I should," he grumbled. "But you'd probably end up in more trouble. Finish your breakfast and coffee, and I'll take you back to your camp."

"Thank you. I don't know how I can repay you. Not at the moment anyhow. But if you give me your phone number or a mailing address, I can send you something. Money, supplies…" She trailed off as he stood abruptly and loomed over her.

"I don't need anything from you."

And with those words, he stomped out of the door.

What did I say to make him seem so angry? Vicky stared at the closed portal wondering but not for long. She had more important issues than a man who didn't seem to know how to interact socially.

Such as, how was she getting out of here? And would he let her go? Despite his claim he'd take her, she had to wonder. And once she got back to camp, what then?

He seemed convinced someone tried to drug her, but who and why?

Chapter Seven

I don't need anything from you.

What a lie. Gene did want something from her, but it wasn't anything as tangible as goods or funds. On the contrary, what he craved was a chance to redo the morning. To take advantage of the naked curves pressed against his. To taste her full lips and put a flush on Vicky's cheeks that had nothing to do with embarrassment but everything to do with arousal.

I'm such a twisted bastard.

He couldn't even rescue a woman without turning it into something about him. But then again, who could blame him? When was the last time he'd lain with a woman? The last time he'd sunk his cock into a woman's welcoming heat and pounded his way to release?

He was horny. Plain and simple. It had nothing to do with this particular woman and everything to do with a man and his normal physical needs. Needs this Vicky could never fulfill.

Only an idiot would miss how timid she was or how she flinched and practically curled in on herself every time he spoke. She acted as if she expected a slap every time she opened her mouth.

Was she truly that much of a mouse? Or had she experienced that kind of abuse at the hands of another?

I'll kill him. Hunt him down, smack him around, and when he's crying for mercy, drag him back to Vicky to show her she never has to fear again. A great plan, but one he wouldn't follow through with because she was none of his business.

Why an urge to protect rose in him, one that had his bear snarling inside his head, he couldn't have said. Vicky and her issues weren't his problem. Her lack of bravery and predilection for fainting when frightened were annoying. The fact someone drugged her coffee, perturbing.

The fact he wanted to keep her, appalling.

Kidnapping for vengeance and ransom was one thing. Keeping a woman to satisfy his needs was not. Only perverts did that.

And very lonely bears.

Other bears maybe, not him.

Gene didn't need anybody. Especially not a short, curvy, myopic, timid, caramel-skinned female who currently poked her head out the door to announce in a low voice, "I'm sorry to bother you, but I was wondering if I was allowed to leave."

Out of curiosity, he queried, "And if I say you're not? That I've changed my mind? That you're staying here?"

Her eyes widened. Not in fright it surprised him to notice, but interest. She ducked her head as she said, "I really shouldn't stay. People will eventually wonder where I am."

"People? No special someone? Friends in the expedition?" Him, fishing for info to see her relationship status? Never. Reconnoitering was just habit.

She shook her head and foolishly answered. "No one. My husband died a while ago. And I've been an orphan since my teens."

He could have smacked her for being so foolish. First rule of survival, never admit to vulnerability. "You mean you came here by yourself?"

She nodded.

"Why?"

"To prove I could." How defensively she uttered it, but also with a hint of defiance.

"To who?"

"Myself. I've never gone on an adventure before."

He could almost admire her reason. "So you chose the harshest place on earth?"

"I wanted to see the polar bears."

He could have shaken her at the answer, especially since it made his bear chuff in pleasure. "So go to a fucking zoo."

"I did. But I wanted to experience more than that. I wanted to see them outside of a cage. Living free."

Funny how the first polar bear she'd found didn't fit that criteria. Gene might have escaped his desert prison, but he'd created his own cage, one of anger and vengeance.

"So is almost getting eaten worth the picture? Was almost dying of exposure worth the little paper you could have written about your arctic adventure?"

She wouldn't meet his eyes and didn't answer.

He sighed. Why did he feel like such a dick? "Get your shit. We're leaving."

No surprise, she didn't reply, just ducked her head back in, but only for a moment before she emerged again, fully dressed, toting her backpack, but her face bare.

"Where are your glasses?"

She shrugged. "Lost. How did you know I wore some?"

"You squint, Pima."

"Pima? My name is Vicky."

"I know what your name is. But I choose to call you Pima. Pain in my ass."

"Well excuse me, Nobody," she sassed back with the first ounce of fire he'd seen in her. A spark shortly lived as she gasped in shock and cringed.

"Oh for fuck's sake. I'm not going to slap you, even if you are a major pain in my ass." Shouldering his own pack, he turned away from her. "Follow me."

Easier said than done. He'd gone only a few dozen yards before he realized he couldn't sense her nearby. He turned around to see her struggling to catch him, her breath panting in the cold air.

He sighed. Short legs on his caramel Pima to his long ones meant he'd have to temper his pace. He should also think about replacing the snowmobile he'd left behind when he'd fled Kodiak Point weeks ago. Going everywhere on foot or paw could prove tiresome, especially when he needed to lug supplies.

But he didn't have the time to go sled shopping now—aka stealing—and if he didn't bring her back, any expedition, even one as poorly run as this one—fucking idiots letting newbies roam around by themselves—would have to report her disappearance and send out a rescue party.

Unless they wanted her dead.

The drugged coffee still bothered him. Vicky claimed she wasn't suicidal, but hearing that her husband had died and seeing how out of place she was out here, he had to wonder. Had he foiled her plan to end her life? Was she so despondent over her mate's death she didn't want to go on?

His gut rejected it. While Vicky appeared timid, he didn't get the impression she was the type to give in to despair. Hints of a possible feisty nature lurked under the surface. There had to be, given the way she'd not only decided to come here in the first place but, despite all that had happened, she never actually freaked out.

Sure she flinched and ducked her head and talked little at times, but honestly, she'd taken things much better than he would have expected. He'd anticipated some hysterics. Maybe some crying, women did so love their tears. Perhaps some yelling. His own mother, that crazy fucking cow, would have screamed like a banshee had she woken up naked in a stranger's embrace.

His Pima? She'd almost seemed disappointed when the cuddling had to end.

Ugh. Had he just used the dreaded C-word? Teddy bears cuddled, polar bears… He didn't know what the fuck his kind did other than maul things for dinner, but it sure as hell wasn't anything so emasculating as cuddling.

In silence, if he ignored her huffing, they approached the embankment edge that led to the lapping sea, and he veered so that they walked parallel to it. Neither of them spoke, but he could feel her glancing at him. Her curious gaze itched at him until he couldn't take it anymore.

"What is it? What do you want to ask?" he snarled.

"N-nothing."

"Vicky…" He growled her name.

"I'm sorry, it's just… You still haven't told me your name. And I wondered what you were doing out here. Are you studying stuff like me?"

"My name is Gene," *but my enemies call me Ghost*. "This is my home." He couldn't believe he told her. Loose lips could get him killed, but then again, he doubted she ran in the type of circles that would care about her rescue by an ornery bastard called Gene. But just in case she did relay her tale to the wrong person, he should probably move on. A shame, he enjoyed the remote location.

"You mean you live here all the time?"

"Most of it. I do spend some time in town, but I prefer the solitude of my hut. I find people annoying."

"Isn't it lonely?"

He almost said yes. "Why do you care?"

"I'm sorry. I don't mean to pry."

"Stop apologizing." He glared at her as he snapped it, and he could see the wall around her coming up, a wall to keep her safe from retaliation. It angered him. "Why are you still flinching? I'm not going to hurt you."

"I can't help it," was her whispered reply.

He wanted to shake her for the inadequate answer, do something, but shit happened.

A peak of ice just behind Vicky exploded into a thousand fragments, and it didn't take his wartime experience to realize someone had just shot at them.

Instantly, his body was in motion, tackling hers to the ground.

She squeaked, "What's happening?"

"Shh. Someone just fired at us."

Facing her for just a moment, he saw her eyes widen, but at least she remained awake.

Two more cracks echoed over the icy plain. They both missed but came close enough to kick up some snow and ice.

"Fuckers," he growled. They were sitting seals out in the open. He needed to get them to cover. "When I say move, you get your round ass behind the hump of ice to your right. Got it?"

She nodded.

As Gene unholstered his gun, he could only hope she'd make it without passing out. He couldn't afford distraction with his enemies intent on harm.

"Ready. Set. Move." He jumped to his feet, his hand gripping the pistol rising and firing in the direction the shots came from. No time to aim. He fired blindly as a cover for Vicky, who scooted behind the short ice hill.

Good girl.

With one worry gone, he tried to focus on the horizon, looking for a speck or movement to indicate where the shooter hid. He didn't spot him immediately, but even dressed in varying shades of white, Gene made a good target.

The next enemy bullet tore a furrow through his jacket and left a bloody gouge along his upper arm. But his enemy had made a mistake. Gene noted the shooter's position.

Off he took running, zigzagging erratically to make himself a harder target. Over and over, he fired his pistol at the enemy's location.

Score! A yelp of pain and the return fire stopped.

A fierce grin split his lips. *I've got you now.*

Actually, what he got was a dead body.

Fuck. Gene stood over the human whose eyes stared sightlessly, the shot to his chest having caused a massive bleed out, which meant no answers. As if Gene needed any.

It seemed the one he'd chosen to quit working for had hired some thugs to try and take him out.

And humans at that. What an insult. As if the Ghost would succumb to such an unworthy opponent.

It will take more than a human to take me down.

Funny how a certain pair of brown eyes came to mind as he thought it. Never, never would he succumb to the allure of a woman. Any woman. No matter how sweet she looked. Despite how she attracted him.

Now if only he could convince his bear, who seemed to think Gene would change his mind if he gave her a few licks.

She's not candy. But he'd bet she tasted sweet.

Dammit, he needed to get rid of her, the sooner, the better—before he did something stupid, like give in to temptation.

Chapter Eight

More bad luck. Vicky truly was plagued, and not just since she'd come on this expedition.

Her run of misfortune had begun months ago, starting with the incident involving the brakes on her car. The mechanic had stated she was lucky to be alive given the fluid in the line had leaked out. The tree she hit didn't fare very well, and neither did the front end of her car. The bruises on her face took weeks to heal because, as it turned out, airbags weren't as soft and cushy as they appeared.

Then there was the carbon monoxide debacle. The bird's nest might have completely blocked the outlet pipe on her gas-powered hot water tank, but the alarm she'd invested in after hearing a story on the news totally saved her life.

Oh and she shouldn't forget the car that sideswiped her when she was out riding her new bike. The poor bush she landed in would never be the same.

It seemed since Rick's death she'd survived more than her fair share of mishaps and now this. Someone shooting at her. Well, technically shooting at her and Gene, but still, there were bullets aimed in her direction.

It was a wonder she remained conscious. She also had to wonder about her rescuer. Her hero was turning out to have a dark side.

Heroes didn't cuss or bark or have guns that they pulled out without a qualm to shoot with. *Less hero, more like villain I think. What have I gotten myself into?* Had she accidentally wandered into something deadly? Was her tough knight some kind of criminal or fugitive? Maybe a drug runner or poacher?

He certainly bore the dangerous look of a man familiar with violence.

"Are you okay?" His sudden reappearance, silent as it was, had her screaming, a cry cut short as he placed a hand over her mouth.

"Shh. We don't know if there are more of them out there. I need you to keep your voice down. Understood?"

She nodded, and he removed his hand. "Why is someone shooting as us?"

"Shooting at me you mean. Let's just say I have enemies."

He didn't elaborate on why he did, though. "Did you find the shooter?" she asked.

He nodded.

She couldn't help but ask, "And?"

"He won't be shooting anymore."

His cold statement left no illusion as to what he meant. She swallowed and fought against the faintness threatening. *Don't you dare pass out now, Victoria Lola Sanchez!* she sternly rebuked herself, and it worked, for now.

"I need to get you back to camp before any of his buddies find us." Gene moved back a pace and held out a hand to help her stand.

As she reached for it, she noted the blood staining the sleeve of his torn coat. "You're hurt," she exclaimed.

"It's nothing."

Nothing to him perhaps, but Vicky didn't do so well with blood. She swayed on her feet.

"Don't you dare face plant on me now," he growled. "Stick with me, Pima."

"I really don't like that name."

"Then prove me wrong and stay upright."

Swallowing against the dizziness, she averted her gaze. "Lead the way."

He did, with a gun in hand. Just the fact that he had one was almost enough to send her into sweet oblivion, but somehow she managed to keep to her feet. One step in front of the other.

She stared at the back of his legs, focused on them to the point of hypnosis. When he stopped, she almost ran into his back. As it was, when he whirled, she'd stopped close enough for an up-close view of his jacketed chest.

"Is that your camp?"

She had to lean around him to peek. The mini tent village rose from the whiteness with a familiarity that signaled safety.

"That's it," she confirmed.

"Then this is where we part ways."

He was leaving? Why did the thought make her sad? Surely, she didn't want to remain with a man who nonchalantly announced people were out to kill him as if it were an everyday occurrence. Apparently she did because she asked, "Will I see you again?"

"No."

How firmly he announced it. Not a maybe. Not even a possibility, which meant she wouldn't have to face him again. But she could already predict he'd revisit her in her dreams. Her usually boring dreams.

If only I had a memory I could look back upon. Something positively daring and exciting. Arousing…

Somehow knowing she'd never have another chance gave her the courage to act. She took him unaware when her hands tugged at his head. He lowered it, and she rose on tiptoes to press her lips against Gene's.

It might have been minus a zillion degrees outside, but that didn't stop the fire that erupted with the kiss. His mouth parted, an exhalation of surprise brushing her lips. She almost drew back, but to her shock, his arms wrapped around her and lifted her. She might have started the embrace, but he took it over. More than that, he moved the kiss to a whole new level. A hot level.

Oh my god. Forget the paltry embraces of her past. *This* was a kiss. This time when she almost swooned it wasn't out of fear, but her first, genuine experience at what true desire felt like.

His mouth slanted over hers, tugging and sucking at her lower lip. She couldn't help a small moan of pleasure. A sound that broke the spell.

Abruptly, she found herself apart from him, standing on wobbly legs, watching as he strode away. No goodbye. No final parting look.

Just a set of tingling lips and a memory she would never forget.

Unlike her camp, which seemed to have forgotten she existed. Heck, they'd never even noted she was gone. She strode into the mini tent city, still somewhat dazed, expecting to have to answer a barrage of questions. On the contrary, the few folks milling around didn't spare her a second look.

No one had noted her absence. No one realized her tent remained empty overnight. No one cared.

She almost cried. The knowledge she had no one who gave a damn was enough to make her wish Gene had kept her after all. At least he seemed to notice her.

But Gene was gone. Forever. Bummer.

And stupid me, I never even got a picture. No matter. His image would probably remain forever imprinted in her mind.

Chapter Nine

Walking away took more effort than it should have. It didn't help that his bear roared at him to go back. It didn't want him to abandon his Pima. It thought Gene should go back for another kiss. And more…

Complete and utter fucking madness.

Gene couldn't offer Vicky anything, other than a fast screw because that was what it would be. Fast. The damned woman ignited all his senses with her bloody innocence.

He couldn't believe she'd mustered up the nerve to kiss him. A clumsy, chaste embrace but still, one freely given. One truly enjoyed. A kiss that burned right through all his protective defenses and made him long for something he couldn't even define.

It was best they split, she back to her camp with its wanna-be adventurers, him to his deadly existence hunted by both friend and foe.

She's better off without me.

So why did it bother him so much? Why did he want to say fuck it and turn around to chase after her? Drag her back to his lair and take what she offered?

He didn't. He kept walking, back to the scene of the shooting, back to the body he'd left behind, looking for answers, but only coming up with more questions.

He found the body where he left it. Frozen and still very dead. A deeper examination of the shooter didn't provide any further clues as to his mission or if he was part of a larger group. The human bore no identification, just off-the-rack mishmashed cold weather gear and the rifle.

In order to keep whomever the dead man might work for guessing, Gene carried the body to the sea edge and tossed it, watching dispassionately as it sank.

Let those who hired him wonder what happened to the man. Let them worry. *Let 'em try again.*

It still nagged at Gene that they'd sent a human. For some reason it just didn't seem right. *He* knew it would take more than an amateur to take the Ghost down. So why waste the money? Or had his previous employer sent out an open bounty call? Would every idiot with a gun set out to hunt him? It would at least break the tedium of his day but seriously cut into his plotting-vengeance time. A vengeance he was less and less inclined to follow through with.

Somewhere along the way, Gene had discovered his anger diminishing. It had started with his encounter with Reid and really snowballed with his confrontation with Boris. A part of him had begun to step back from the dark emotions within to perceive events from another view.

For so long he'd blamed his former brother soldiers for not trying harder to find him when they escaped. For not rescuing him. When they said they didn't know he lived, that they would have moved heaven and earth to save him if they'd known, he heard the truth in their words. Saw it in their faces.

Can I honestly say I would have done any differently than them?

He didn't like the answer. But no longer blaming his old friends didn't mean he was ready to beg for forgiveness and acceptance into their fucking Kumbaya—let's all love each other—clan. Gene still preferred solitude to the inane chattering of people.

Pima doesn't chatter.

Fuck him, how had his thoughts returned to her? Yes, Vicky might not irritate him with nonstop blabbing, but he did dislike her timid nature. The woman needed to stand up for herself. Predators preyed on the weak, thrived on inaction and demure acceptance. If she wouldn't protect herself, then she should look into getting someone who would.

Like me.

No, not him. He had no use for a human girl afraid of her own shadow. Besides, with him gone, there was no one to make demands of her or frighten her into submission. By her account, her husband was dead, and hopefully she'd prove smart enough to stay away from that kind of abusive dick in the future. She was here alone, safe from harm if she stayed away from hunted polar bears—and coffee. The reminder that someone had tried to harm her returned to nag at him.

Gene believed her when she said she'd not drugged her own beverage. But if not her, then who, and why? Why would someone want to harm a hair on her cute little head?

Cute? Ack. Where did that thought come from? He almost gave himself a slap, but he didn't want to lose his train of thought.

What if he had it wrong? What if the sleeping agent wasn't supposed to put her asleep when she went for a walk and let her slip into a cold, painless death? What if someone meant to place her in a deep repose while she was in camp? Alone. Defenseless in her tent.

Vicky was attractive. What man in their right mind wouldn't want to touch her soft, caramelized skin? Kiss those luscious, full lips? Hold on to those plentiful curves as he…

A growl rumbled from him, and not just him, his bear.

No touch. She's mine.

Such a possessive declaration, which held no grounds. Yes, she'd kissed him. Probably a thank you, which he'd exploited—*because I'm such a greedy a-hole.*

But that's all it was. A kiss. A kiss that still burned his lips. A kiss that tasted of innocence, which was foolish. Vicky had admitted she was married. So she was definitely not a virgin. Yet, something in the way she embraced, the hesitation and uncertainty screamed of inexperience.

I'd love to teach her.

But he wouldn't. And he wouldn't let anyone steal that sweet innocence from her either.

Given someone had already made on attempt to incapacitate her, chances were they'd make a second. He should get her away from the camp. His bear agreed and took it one step further and suggested they bring her back to their den.

Bad plan, on so many levels. For one thing, with him attacked, Gene could only assume his hut was compromised. The other reason his bear's plan wouldn't work was he didn't trust himself alone with

Vicky. Especially if there was a bed nearby. A man had only so much restraint when it came to an attractive woman, and with her having shown such willingness in her kiss, his resistance to her charms was debatable.

What to do then? He couldn't trust himself alone with her, yet he couldn't leave her unattended and defenseless.

Big sigh. Again. It seemed he had a never-ending supply of those where she was concerned and to think he'd known her only twenty-four hours.

With no clear plan other than the one that insisted he offer her protection, Gene gave in to his bear's idea.

Stashing his gear in a hollow he dug in the snow, he swapped shapes and lumbered to a promontory that gave him a nice view of the camp. If he couldn't be around her as a man, then he'd watch over her as his beast.

He'd blend in better that way.

And probably scare the piss out of anyone who might try and broach her tent if he went charging in full polar mode at them.

A bear's got to have some fun.

Chapter Ten

It still miffed Vicky that no one seemed to have noted her absence. Not even the tour guide. Was he so lax in his responsibilities that he didn't bother to keep even a general eye on his charges?

The only person who really seemed interested in her reappearance was one of the creepy guys, the one she'd labeled Mullet—yes, the hair style was still alive and well, at least on this dude. It wasn't the most attractive style, but it wasn't as awful as how he made her skin crawl.

When she exited her tent to swap her empty water jug for a full one, his gaze followed her. She kept her eyes averted, got what she needed and scurried back. The fresh water wasn't to make coffee though. Gene's assertion that hers was drugged still bothered her, and she still wasn't entirely sure she believed him.

Who would want to drug her? And how had they done it? She'd made the coffee herself from her jar of coffee crystals. No one had a chance to tamper with it, or so she thought. Yet, given her loopiness and fatigue, which, while possibly attributable to her almost freezing to death situation, did seem odd given she didn't recall being particularly cold when the drowsiness first set in.

Whatever the reason for her glacier nap, she was steering clear of the instant crystals in favor of sealed juice-flavored sugar. In a cup she rinsed out beforehand, just in case. *If it's good enough for astronauts, it's good enough for me.* It didn't make it taste any better, though, she thought, making a face at the sweet concoction.

With nothing better to do, she sat down on her cot and proceeded to dump out her knapsack, which contained her phone—which mocked her with its two service bars—and camera among other things. Some kind of intrepid explorer she was turning out to be. While she'd snapped a few pictures of her bear encounter, she'd not managed to get any of the man who rescued her.

A man who used his body to protect her from gunfire. A dangerous guy she dared to kiss—and who kissed her back.

Sigh.

For a guy she'd spent only a few hours with, she certainly missed his gruff nature. How she wished she'd gotten to spend more time with him, which was totally crazy.

The man was a stranger, one involved in some kind of violent thing, given people were shooting at him, and if Gene could be believed, he'd taken care of their attacker, permanently.

She shivered. *He admits to being a killer, and yet that doesn't frighten me.* On the contrary, his dark side attracted her, which was taking her new adventure motto too far.

Coming on this expedition had been meant to expand her horizons, not end them as a dead bystander caught in the crossfire of some kind of arctic war.

But she was worrying about nothing. Gene was gone. As in not coming back, out of her life, never to be seen again. The only thing she would ever have of him was a memory.

Bummer.

A touch hungry, she went to fire up her propane stove, only to realize her tank was empty. She'd have to swap it out for a fresh one.

Exiting her tent, she practically ran into Mullet. She halted with a mumbled, "Sorry, I didn't see you there." With the tent at her back, she couldn't quite give herself space, and he didn't seem inclined to step away.

"How did you get here?"

What an odd thing to ask. She wrinkled her nose. "Excuse me. I don't quite understand what you mean. I came here with everyone else. Remember, I was the one who got to piggyback with our guide and fell off." The lurch of the snowmobile when they'd first set off took her by surprise to everyone's vast entertainment. But the true embarrassment was when she was relegated to riding in one of the sleds with raised sides along with the supplies. Sure it was probably safer, and admittedly easier for her, but her cheeks burned at the public admission that she was a klutz.

It seemed Mullet wasn't done with his odd line of questioning. "That's not what I meant. I meant, didn't you go out exploring?"

Someone noticed! A pity he was someone she preferred to not have watching her. "I did."

"Anything *interesting* happen?"

Tons, but she wasn't about to tell him about it. "Nope. Nothing. Just lots and lots of ice and snow." And a bear and a man and a shooter.

Mullet stared at her suspiciously with his beady eyes, and she fidgeted. But when she didn't say anything more, he grunted and walked away.

A breath whistled out from her. She hadn't even realized she held it. *What a weird guy.* One she would steer clear of. Why the sudden interest in her whereabouts?

She took back her earlier annoyance over no one noting her absence. She'd prefer to remain in obscurity than have creepy guys like Mullet and his friends pay her any mind.

Once he left, things returned to normal. Much like an invisible spirit, she wandered through camp to switch out her propane tank, no one paying her any mind. Out of curiosity she asked their tour guide, who was tinkering once again with a snowmobile engine, "Does anybody manage to live out here?"

"Look around you."

"No, I mean live, as in permanently."

"There's still some tribes who do. The hunting is good, and they can follow the old ways without bureaucrats and red tape getting in their way."

"But what about non-natives?" she persisted. "I mean, surely there are some permanent residents?"

The guide stopped his work to give her a hard stare. "Listen, I don't know what you're getting at or why you care, but whatever the reason, stay out of it. Or more specifically, stay away from them. Yes, there's people living out here. And most don't like cidiots butting their curious noses into their affairs. If you know what's good for you, you'll stick to what you came for, studying the wildlife. I might also suggest not wandering off by yourself, neither. Bad things can happen to those who don't practice precaution."

"You knew I was gone?" She couldn't help an accusatory note. "Why didn't you come looking for me?"

"I did. Saw someone got to you first."

"And didn't bother to come for me or notify anyone?" How rude. What if Gene had been a man with less honor?

"I wasn't about to tangle with *him*."

"Him? Do you mean Gene?" she asked.

"Enough with the questions. I'm done answering. And you need to stop asking. Count yourself lucky that you're back here and, like I said, no more wandering off. Next time you might not end up so fortunate."

More confused than ever, Vicky returned to her tent. What did the guide mean? Was he inferring Gene had a less-than-stellar reputation? Surely the man who saved her wasn't so bad.

While she could only fantasize various scenarios—from Gene being the outcast son of some kind of arctic family to a one-man, Rambo-like recluse—they did keep her entertained the rest of the day. More out of boredom than anything else, she went to bed early that night and hoped for a reoccurrence of dreams featuring a certain naked man.

The sounds in the camp lulled her, the murmur of voices, a radio softly playing, the rumble of the generator when it kicked a background hum to them all. The various noises kept her awake as her mind slowly shut down. Eventually, the residents around her settled in for the night and she finally drifted off.

While she didn't hear a thing, she certainly felt the cold draft that caressed her exposed face.

What on earth—

A hand slapped over her mouth and a menacing voice warned, "Not a sound."

As if she could scream with him muffling her.

But as to his added, "Don't move."

Not a problem. With sudden fear invading every inch of her body, she could feel the faintness coming on.

No. No. I mustn't pass out now. God only knew what would happen to her or where she'd wake up. Unlike her experience with Gene, she didn't get the impression the guy holding her hostage meant her well. If she let her terror overpower her, she might never wake again.

Fighting the lassitude trying to blanket her mind didn't mean she expended energy pushing back the inertia of her body. As her assailant dragged her from her cot, she left her limbs limp. Heavy. Let him exert himself if he wanted to kidnap her.

His grunt of exertion helped to ease some of her fright. Whoever accosted her definitely lacked Gene's effortless strength. She began to think she could maybe fight her way loose until he said, "Mind giving me a fucking hand here? The heifer weighs a goddamned ton."

Heifer? Vicky might sport a few extra pounds, but calling her a cow was totally uncalled for. Oddly enough the comment sparked a teensy tiny flare of anger.

"You heard what the boss said. You need to drag her. We're supposed to make it look like a bear snagged her."

What the heck were they talking about? What boss and why did they want to cover up their tracks by blaming a poor defenseless polar bear?

"Are you finished slashing the back of her tent?" grumbled the one holding her.

"Almost. Fucking shit is tougher to cut than my old lady's meatloaf."

With her faint spell having passed by, and the comments clicking together in her mind, Vicky came to a startling conclusion.

These guys want me dead.

The spark in her flared brighter, and suddenly his order to remain quiet and obedient, yeah, that wasn't working for her. Vicky began to struggle. Twisting in his grip, taking him by surprise enough that the hand covering her mouth slipped, and she managed a short, "Help!" before a fist connected with her jaw.

Ooh look at the pretty colored spots.

Dazed and her cheek throbbing, Vicky lay on the floor, squinting in the gloom, straining to grasp what was happening. The soft glow of her nightlight let her see two, or was that three, figures looming over her. Nope, it was just one, Shorty, friends with Mullet, who was currently wielding a knife and shredding her tent.

Before she could gather her wits to yell again, fabric was stuffed into her mouth, and Shorty booted her in the ribs with a snapped, "Don't make this any harder than it has to be."

Well excuse me for not going quietly to my death.

What do you know? She had an ounce of spunk in her after all. Gene would have been so proud. Pity she'd have little time to celebrate it.

Hole accomplished in the back of her tent—which cost her a small fortune!—they seemed intent on dragging her out of it, in her nightclothes where she'd probably freeze to death before they had a chance to kill her.

"Wait a second," whispered Shorty. "If we're supposed to make this look like a bear got her shouldn't we have some blood? You know, on account of the claws and stuff."

Her eyes widened, and not just because the pair turned to look at her, the silver gleam of the knife in Mullet's hand ominous.

Worrisome, but it paled in comparison to another problem.

It seemed they wouldn't need to fake her demise by polar bear because looming over them was her friend from the sea ledge. Old Scarface himself, which funnily enough made her think of Gene, who also sported a similar identifying mark.

The towering polar menace opened his mouth but waited until the two wanna-be murderers turned to peek at what had her goggling in fright.

The polar bear roared, and this time, Vicky didn't fight the faint but dove toward it.

Chapter Eleven

Not for the first time, Gene questioned what the hell he was doing spying on Vicky's tent. She wasn't his concern.

She needs our protection.

No, she was a distraction he could ill afford.

She was a temptation that called to him.

She was…under attack?

While a part of him had used the excuse of guarding her as a reason to remain nearby, another part of him never truly believed she was in danger. Yet, there was no denying that the dark figure at the back of the tent, busily slicing at the fabric, meant no good.

The perpetrator also wasn't alone, or so the brief scream abruptly cut short indicated. Gene didn't need to hear Vicky's cry of distress to get moving. At the first sign of trouble, his bear ass was lumbering down the icy hillock he'd chosen as his watchtower.

I should have never left her alone. He should have known better. His enemies must have spotted his interaction with Vicky and now sought to use her against him. *Like fuck.* He'd soon show them the error of their ways. *No mercy. No second chance.*

Arriving at the bottom of the slope, he treaded more cautiously, intent on taking the arguing pair by surprise.

Vicky lay at their feet, half in, half out of the tent, eyes wide with fright—*look at that, she's still awake!*—while the bastards discussed bleeding her to make it seem like a polar attack. Oh the irony.

I'll show them what a real polar attack looks like.

On silent paws, Gene approached and stood. He noted the moment Vicky saw him. It caught the bastards' attention too. They turned. Their jaws dropped. He saw the whites of their eyes, which practically popped from their heads.

And when he roared? At least one of them pissed himself.

Awesome.

But not as awesome as the pleasure he got out of swiping at them with paws tipped in curved claws.

"Holy—" was all one got to say before Gene's blow sent him flying while the other one tried to dive back into Vicky's damaged tent. He didn't move fast enough. Gene yanked him, and while he preferred a fresh sea catch as a meal, in this case, he made an exception. It took only a chomp to end that life.

But he didn't stop to enjoy this fresh snack. Not with the other one trying to crawl away while screaming, "Bear! There's a fucking bear! Someone help me."

Pussy. A brave man when attacking a defenseless women, but put him face to face with a real predator and his true colors emerged. As did some of the tent city occupants. Lucky for him, most stared in stunned disbelief. It wouldn't last though. It would only take one yahoo grabbing a gun to turn this into a bigger fucking mess.

Dropping to all four paws, Gene ignored his last target in order to return to Vicky, who lay still as a statue.

Apparently she'd reached the end of her brave tether and slept through the resulting chaos.

Lights came on throughout the camp as voices called to each other, the ominous words, "Get the tranquilizer gun" and "Screw that, where's my rifle?" cropping up.

The hill that previously hid him wouldn't provide concealment if he tried to climb it. Sauntering through camp to exit it would probably not go unnoticed.

What was a bear to do when faced with a bunch of panicked humans with weapons?

Gene had just beaten a retreat into Vicky's damaged tent, with her draped on his naked lap, when a grizzled face poked into the hole.

His blue gaze met the brown-eyed one of a wolf. Not a word was spoken but the yells outside continued.

"Where's the damned bear? I've got a surprise for it!" hollered someone outside.

"You can't kill it," yelled another. "They're a protected species."

"Where did it go?" shrilled a woman.

Gene watched the guide, ready to lunge if needed to silence him. The other male gave him a slight nod before shouting, "Everyone get back in your tents and sit tight while I scout."

A nod of thanks was owed for that.

"That will give us a few minutes, long enough for you to tell me who you are," said the older shifter.

"No one you want to mess with," Gene replied in a low growl.

The whiskered fellow raised a brow. "Perhaps not, and yet, I have to question your presence here. This is my camp, and this girl is one of my charges."

Gene's presence had everything to do with the Pima on his lap, not that he'd admit it out loud. But the old guy wanted an answer. "Think of me as her guardian fucking angel."

The fellow in charge of the camp, a role Gene had deciphered during his hours of observation, snorted. "Most vicious angel I ever met. I reckon the dead one and the one screaming bloody murder were up to no good."

"They were up to something all right."

The other man's gaze narrowed. "I've heard of you. You're the one they call Ghost."

Why answer when a feral smile would do the trick.

Interestingly enough, it didn't daunt the old coot. "Are you going to harm the girl?"

"Wasn't planning to." Gene couldn't have said what he planned other than he wouldn't let anyone lay a finger on her with ill intent. He'd bite it off first.

The wolf grunted. "Oddly enough, I believe you. But you can't stay here."

"No shit."

"Neither can she."

Say what? "Why not?"

The old guy gave him a look.

"She's an innocent," Gene exclaimed. In more ways than one.

"Not anymore I'd say. Whatever is going on, she's now a part of it, and I can't keep her safe. You need to take her away from here."

No, no and no. This wasn't part of his plan. *I don't want to be saddled with her.* And the old wolf couldn't force him.

Gene should dump her ass on the floor, get up, and walk away. The old guy couldn't stop him. He had to be wrong. If Gene removed himself, then Vicky would…

Dammit. The old man was right. She wasn't safe. Not anymore. Still though, to take her with him? He didn't need the annoyance of caring for her sweet ass. Bad guys weren't supposed to be responsible for anyone but themselves. So he was surprised to hear himself say, "I need transportation."

All the arguments in the world and it boiled down to he couldn't let her come to harm because of him. Bloody chivalrous side. It would emerge at the most inopportune time.

Since when do I have fucking morals, and how do I get rid of them? Morals got in the way of violence and revenge. And Gene did so enjoy dishing out violent vengeance.

"You can take the snowmobile these fellows used to come in. The sledge is still hooked to it. It has some supplies still on board and room for her."

Help? What an odd concept. "Why are you doing this?" Suspicion, always a friend, especially when things appeared too good to be true.

"I know why you're hiding, Ghost."

Gene tensed. Someone who knew his secrets? He'd kill the old guy if he had to.

"I'm not going to tell anyone, boy, so calm down. And when I said I know you're hiding I wasn't referring to your reputation or the trouble you've gotten embroiled in. See, boy, I was you forty years ago. A son of a bitch angry at the world, determined to make them pay and never let anyone get close."

"And? Seems to have worked for you. You're still alive and kicking."

"Alive yes. Happy no. Don't make the same mistakes I did. Don't let the ghosts of the past take away your future. Life is too short for bitterness and recriminations. You still have a chance for happiness."

"There is no redemption for me."

"Forgiveness can happen to anyone, if you learn to forgive yourself."

Funny how his words almost echoed Boris'. Gene didn't reply, but he did notice himself absently stroking the soft skin of Vicky's cheek. He snatched his hand away, but not before the old wolf noticed.

"You still have a chance. Don't fuck it up. Take your woman and go. Find somewhere safe."

"She's not my woman."

The old guy snorted. "If you say so. Whatever she is to you, she doesn't deserve to die because of it."

"She won't die." A fierce claim said aloud, which made it binding. Fucking morals again. *I thought I ditched those bastards in that prison.*

"If you want to make sure she stays alive then you better get moving before the other boys realize you're here still."

More little bastards who wanted to harm a defenseless woman? Not just his bear bristled at the thought. "How many more in the group?"

"Two, unless the third one who left yesterday is coming back."

Gene's malevolent smile answered that.

"Then only two, but they're armed and tougher than this pair."

"Shifter?" Gene said it aloud. It wasn't as if the old guy didn't know what Gene was. If his polar bear could tell with one sniff, then the grizzled wolf surely knew.

"Human, but military trained. They won't panic like those idiots."

In other words, maybe a little more of a challenge. Excellent. Gene did enjoy a good fight. "What are you going to tell authorities?" Because no way could the expedition leader hide the fact several of his group had gone missing.

A crooked smile split the wolf's lips. "I'll tell them the truth. Bear attack. One killed, another injured, and the poor little lady here is missing."

A rare grin ghosted his lips. "I assume at one point she'll surface, having miraculously survived because a brave hunter rescued her and brought her to civilization."

"Something like that. I'm sure you'll figure something out. Enough chatter. You best get her dressed and moving. Where's your clothes?"

"Stashed a ways from here."

"I've got some stuff you can use. It might be a bit tight, but at least you won't freeze. You'll have to stay hidden though until you reach them, you and the girl. I'll stash the garments with the sled. First, though, I gotta get the folks here looking the other way whilst you escape."

The wolf retreated from the tent, leaving Gene alone with Vicky, who, despite her trembling from the cold and a blossoming bruise on her cheek—*Grrr*—seemed relatively unharmed, but not out of danger if the old wolf could be believed.

I'll keep you safe.

In order to accomplish that, though, he needed to get her out of here before the pricks with guns showed their ugly human faces to finish the job. But he couldn't exactly drag her out in her onesie flannel jammies patterned with… He peered in disbelief. Frolicking polar bears.

"The woman is demented." But in a cute way. She was also regaining consciousness.

"What happened?" she asked groggily. Her eyes fluttered open, and she caught sight of him. Most women would have screamed. She gasped, a soft feminine sound he could have gobbled up, especially since it had his name. "Gene. What are you doing here?"

"What's it look like I'm doing?" *Being a fucking idiot.* "I'm saving you from danger. Again. You're a damned magnet, Pima. Leave you alone for a few hours and you just can't stay out of trouble."

She bit her lower lip. "I didn't do it on purpose."

"Sure you didn't," he groused. He knew she didn't, just like she didn't purposely try to rouse his lusty side with the innocent nibble of that delectable lip. Either way, it still had him doing and feeling things he shouldn't.

It also had him thinking, *Hey, there's a bed, and I'm naked, she could be naked and…*

Not the time. Not the place. Not the woman he had any right to lust after.

Dumping Vicky on the bed, he stood. Spotting her knapsack, he grabbed it and began to stuff anything that looked useful into it. The old wolf had said he'd provide a diversion. When it hit, he needed them ready to move.

"I swear I didn't do anything. I was sleeping when those guys came in and attacked me. Speaking of which—" She sat up and peeked around myopically. "Where are they?" As she asked, she blindly groped for a set of glasses that sat on a latched box and perched them on her nose.

Damn. No woman with her cute factor should be allowed to wear dark-rimmed glasses with hair tumbled around their shoulders and lips ready for a kiss. It was much too distracting.

"They're gone." He found a pair of wool socks and wedged them on his feet. But he doubted any of her garments would fit his broad shoulders or thick thighs.

"Did my bear get them?"

Her bear? Funny how he liked the sound of that. "He did."

"Good."

Good? Had his timid Pima said good? "Excuse me? Since when is a bear attack considered a good thing?"

"Did you know those jerks were planning to kill me and wanted to make it look like a bear attack? I'm glad Karma paid them back."

His sweet Pima vehement about vengeance? Shiver. *Why must she say the most arousing things?* "Yeah, Karma got them, but now their friends might retaliate."

"What do you mean?" Before he could reply, she finally seemed to notice a few important facts. The first being… "Gene, why are you naked?"

Luckily, he had a ready-made answer. "I had to ditch my clothes."

"But why? It's cold."

"I know, but they were covered in blood, you know from the bear attack. I thought it best to rid myself of them in case it brought your hungry polar back." Little did she know it wasn't blood that would draw him to her but her innate sweetness. *Argh*.

She blinked at his reply, but didn't swallow it. A shame. "Back up a second. I guess the first questions I should have asked are why are you here in the first place and how were you close enough to get covered in blood? You didn't wrestle with the bear, did you?"

"Only an idiot wrestles with a polar."

"Speaking of which, what happened to my bear? You didn't hurt him, did you?"

Honestly, Gene probably hurt himself everyday letting his anger run his life. But he didn't have time for mind-shrinking bullshit and her questions. "Would you stop with the interrogation and get dressed? We have to go."

"Go, go where?" she queried but at the same time acted, suiting herself in her winter gear.

"Away."

"But why?"

"Dammit, Pima. Would you stop it with the questions? Your ass is in danger, and I'm going to save it, against my better fucking judgment. So unless you'd prefer to end up going home in a body bag, just do what I say. Quietly."

Her lips clamped shut, and a hurt expression flashed across her face. He wanted to punch himself. Here she showed signs of spirit and he squashed it.

She can get feisty later, once we've gotten away from here and I know she's safe.

The questions stopped, and she quickly dressed, turning her back to him to strip off her jammies, leaving her clad in form-fitting long johns—which he found way sexier than normal—over which she layered proper clothing for the elements. What a shame she had to hide those curves.

Get your head in the game and stop lamenting the fact she's covering up her delectable body. Given things could explode at any moment, he needed to put his time to good use. In other words, he needed to find some kind of clothing. However, he doubted anything in her tent would fit. It took but a simple yank to tear a hole in her sleeping bag, which he then tossed over his head poncho style. He would have preferred going bear, but he wasn't quite ready to reveal that side of himself to Vicky. Especially since the shock would probably result in her face planting.

A gun shot went off, a loud boom that generated a few screams and yells. "The bear's on the east side of the camp." No he wasn't, but Gene recognized a diversion when he heard one.

"That's our cue. Follow right behind me."

He ignored the front flap in favor of the man-made opening at the rear. Out the tattered back of the tent he crept, alert for anyone who might not have fallen for the plot to avert attention. Along the outer edge of the camp he snuck, Vicky a panting shadow at his back, fear making her breathe harshly, but at least she remained upright.

While the yells continued from the other end of the encampment, and the occasional gunshot echoed, their side remained relatively quiet.

Too quiet.

Too easy.

Gene didn't like it.

He halted in the shadow of the last tent, able to see the silent snowmobiles parked at random. He might have wondered which one the old wolf meant for him to take if he hadn't spotted the pile of clothing on the seat of one of them.

Fuck me. If I get out of this alive, I'm going to owe the old guy a favor. How about by not killing him because he knows who I am? That seemed fair. The villain handbook never advocated allies. Allies would eventually betray you. But, once upon a time, Gene recalled when that wasn't true. When he used to run with a set of men who would have laid their lives down for him. Until he let his messed-up emotions fuck with their lives.

Forget the past. Here and now, there was only him, and one severely frightened human.

He crouched down in the shadow of the last tent, and Vicky followed suit. He whispered, "I'm going to go out there first. Alone. I want to see if anyone is watching the sleds. I'll start the engine, and if the coast is clear, I'll wave you over. You come running and hop into the sledge."

"Not behind you?"

"Can you promise not to faint if someone chases after us and starts to shoot?"

"Sled it is," she replied with a wry grin and cute wrinkle of her nose.

Again, another pesky smile ghosted his lips. If he wasn't careful, he'd actually end up enjoying himself. *Can't have that happening.* It would totally ruin his reputation.

While leaving Vicky alone wasn't ideal, he needed to ensure there wasn't a trap waiting for him. The old wolf might seem like the honest sort, but if the other humans hunting were even slightly skilled, they'd recognize the diversionary tactic.

Which meant he might be walking into danger.

Awesome. And him wearing a fucking sleeping bag as a poncho, bare legs poking out the bottom. How emasculating.

His bear ducked its head in his mind and put paws over its eyes. Add embarrassing too. He contented himself with the knowledge he could kill anyone who dared mock him and before they could recount what they saw.

But what about Vicky? She'd know.

He'd deal with her loose lips later. *By plastering mine against them and making her swear secrecy. We'll seal it with a kiss. Or two.*

Or not. *Get your head into the fucking game.* Thoughts of seduction did not mesh with getting out alive.

His feet almost numb with cold, he dashed out to the snowmobile and ducked beside it. Ears and eyes alert, he scanned the area as he tugged on the gear, mismatched odds and ends that were tight across his shoulders, but would do. The boots, however, those wouldn't go on his gigantic feet. However the old guy had left him two pairs of thermal socks, and given the sled had hand and feet warmers, it should keep him from losing any important body parts.

The last thing he found was the true treasure. A magnum gun. Fully loaded. *Make that two favors I owe him.* Any gun guy could see the weapon was a well-loved classic, and yet the old coot had left it for him.

Tucking it in his waistband, Gene straddled the snowmobile and turned the key. Primed and ready to go, the engine rumbled to life. No one came running. No one screamed a warning. No one took a shot.

He still didn't like it.

Half turning in his seat, he signaled for Vicky to join him. Graceful did not describe her. She ran like a girl. A girl who hated running. A girl with two left feet who went plunging to the ground as they tangled.

Her clumsiness saved her life.

Chapter Twelve

Ever since she'd woken, Vicky had moved on autopilot, still bemused by the series of events assailing her.

The attack on her person and subsequent rescue by her bear, while mind boggling enough, weren't the only reasons for her lack-witted state.

Gene was back. Gene came to save her. Gene was once again naked. *Drool.*

Gene. Gene. Gene.

Considering how little time she'd known him, the man kept appearing just when she most needed him. *Like a guardian angel.* Kind of like her polar bear.

Funny how many traits the two shared, from their uncanny knack to appear when her life was in peril to the fact they were both big and mean looking and, in a weird coincidence, shared a similar facial scar. They were also, beneath their growly toughness, softies where she was concerned. She considered the fact the two deadly predators hadn't killed her a sign. A sign of what, she couldn't say. She just knew that she could trust them.

So when Gene told her to get dressed and follow, she did. When he told her to stick to the shadows and wait for his signal, she waited. When he told her to run, she ran. If only her body would cooperate.

To her undying embarrassment, she once again proved her ineptitude by tripping over her own feet and landing face first on the packed snow. The good news, her glasses survived the impact and remained on her face. The bad news, her dignity was squashed.

Which turned out to be a good thing.

"Stay down," Gene yelled. "Someone's shooting at us."

Sure enough, he'd no sooner announced it than something hit the snow inches from her head, spraying her with tiny particles of ice.

Before she could yelp, or faint, Gene was there, hauling her to her feet and firing a weapon of his own into the darkness.

How did he go from naked to dressed and armed? The man kept surprising her with his versatility, not to mention his cool head. Someone was shooting at them, and he didn't seem the least bit afraid. Was there anything that daunted him?

"Stop daydreaming, Pima, and move."

He didn't have to tell her twice. She ran the rest of the way to the sled as Gene popped off another round. It was answered, the reply shot whizzing just over her head as she stumbled.

Lucky again. But how long before her luck ran out?

"Get in the sled and duck down."

No problem. Vicky scooted into the open spot among the bundles and hung low, not even daring to peer over the edges. She did gulp, though, as something hit the sledge and punched a hole in its side. It missed her but lodged in one of the packages.

"Hold on. I'm going to get us out of here," Gene announced as he hopped onto the snowmobile and gunned it. With a loud roar from the engine, the snowmobile took off, the sudden lurch sending her teetering. She fell against the bundles at her rear, but stayed there, fear freezing her limbs.

But, hey, I'm awake.

For now. With icy terror running through her veins, Vicky knew she'd have to rein in her emotions or risk passing out again, which might not be a good idea.

I have to remain conscious. For some reason this mattered, whether to prove to herself she could face calamity or to show Gene she wasn't dead weight. It didn't matter what the reason. She had to stop letting her problems overwhelm her. Time to start facing things, even unpleasant ones, eyes open.

The gunfire seemed to have ceased, but still Vicky didn't dare sit up. Bravery didn't mean acting stupid. Gene said to stay low, and as he was a guy who appeared to have survived worse situations than this, she'd trust his judgment. After all, because of him, she wasn't dead, yet, despite the many attempts.

And what the heck was that about?

Surely whoever hated Gene wasn't so desperate as to keep targeting her? It made no sense. The guys in her expedition who'd gone after her didn't even know she'd met him when they signed on. But Mullet had suspected something when she came back from her overnight adventure.

It put their conversation in a whole new light. Had Hairy and Mullet, or the rest of their gang, spied upon her chance meeting with Gene?

Had they come along with the group as some kind of cover to their underlying mission of hunting out Gene and killing him?

Gulp. *What have I gotten involved in?*

And why couldn't she keep from thinking it was the most exciting thing to have ever happened to her? Almost as exciting as Gene's kiss—and hot, naked butt.

Just when she thought they'd escaped danger and she could breathe easy, lights caught them, a pair, bobbing and bouncing and closing in behind them. Gene gunned the motor to little effect. Weighted down with the sled, which didn't just carry supplies but one chubby Latina—who really enjoyed her second helpings—he couldn't hope to outrun the chasing pair.

"Fuck!" Gene's expletive came to her even over the sound of rushing wind and the engine. "Hold on tight, Pima. Things are about to get rough."

Okay, maybe now was a good time to pass out, and before she threw up the contents of her tummy because he wasn't kidding about rough. The snowmobile sloughed to the left then the right, sending the sledge fishtailing.

She closed her eyes tight and flattened herself as much as she could on the bottom. *I've been on worse roller coaster rides.* But those lasted only a minute or so. This went on and on.

Shots rang out, sharp cracks and not just from those chasing behind them. Through a peeping eye, she saw a muzzle flash as Gene, half turned in his seat, returned fire. Thank goodness out here on the icy plains they didn't have to worry about trees. But there were uneven humps.

They hit one, and for a moment, Vicky floated, airborne, before slamming back down among the bundles with an oomph.

"Oops," Gene said, sounding apologetic.

It almost made Vicky laugh. She bit back a hysterical giggle, which was better than a sob. Not that she was close to crying; on the contrary, she was wide-awake, hanging on for dear life and praying the next bump they hit wouldn't tip them.

To think, only a few hours ago she was bored out of her mind. For a girl who didn't particularly enjoy action flicks, she was certainly living one. *I would have preferred falling into a romantic comedy. One with a beach, sand, and Gene accidentally losing his bathing suit and emerging from some waves.*

Despite that, she couldn't say she was hating the adventure. Being with Gene, even under attack, beat the doldrums of hanging out alone in her tent. Maybe once they lost their pursuers they'd have a chance to cuddle again. To keep warm of course. Maybe kiss. As a thank-you. Or she could try something more daring.

Pop. The latest round that whistled overhead deflated that pleasant bubble of thought.

"I can't outrun them," Gene announced over his shoulder. "We're going to have to stop and let them catch us."

"What? Are you out of your mind? Those guys are trying to kill us." Forget trusting him, she questioned his crazy idea.

"Exactly. So I'll just have to kill them first."

Said without the slightest hesitation. "You're nuts." She breathed it under her breath.

He should have never heard it over noise of the engine, but apparently he caught it because he replied. "Nuts? More like psychotic. Or, as my therapist used to say, incapable of channeling my anger and acting out inappropriately."

He called killing people acting inappropriately? *And this is the man in whose hands I'm placing my life?*

Maybe she was the one in need of a therapist.

Gene cut the engine before they'd come to a full stop and, with their momentum, spun the snowmobile so it faced the oncoming headlights. She didn't need his shouted advice of, "Keep your head down," to tuck it between her trembling knees.

Breathe in. Breathe out. She concentrated on that simple task as the rumble of motors got louder. Closer. Scarier.

She clenched her eyes tight, almost wishing oblivion would take her before a heart attack did.

Bang.

With a sputter, one of the snowmobiles croaked. One pursuer taken out of the equation, leaving only the single whine of an engine pushed hard.

Boom.

The second snowmobile didn't die, but given the human scream of pain, it seemed fairly evident the driver might.

Nausea had her swallowing and fighting to hold on to the roiling liquid in her tummy.

The crunch of snow had her rousing enough to lift her head in time to spot Gene heading toward both sets of headlights.

What's he doing?

Going after them, dummy, just like he said he would.

Given the gun in his hand, he wouldn't ask them nicely to go away.

Gulp.

The dead sled still had power, but wasn't moving anywhere. The other, with the incapacitated driver, rumbled drunkenly but, given the angle of the light, appeared to have tipped on to its side.

Much like a gawker at the scene of an accident, Vicky couldn't help but watch events unfold, eyes peeking over the edge, fingers clinging to the side. She stared, barely breathing as Gene bravely stalked toward the vehicles. Walked stupidly into danger given the lone figure that stood atop his snowmobile and shouted, "Just give us the girl. She's the one we want."

Me? They want me? For some reason that didn't give her a warm, fuzzy feeling inside. Where was wallflower obscurity when a girl needed it?

"And if I do hand her over, you'll leave me alone?" Gene asked.

What? He wasn't seriously contemplating giving her to those thugs? After all he'd done to save her? But then again, could she blame him? If they were in fact after her instead of him—incredible as it seemed—then why risk his life?

"The job we were given only mentions the girl. We got no bone to pick with you."

"What job?" Gene asked as he stood in the bright glare of the headlight, gun held loosely by his side, his entire attitude one of relaxed nonchalance.

Vicky, on the other hand, shook like a leaf in the wind, her teeth chattered, and she really wished she'd had time to go potty before embarking on this madness.

It seemed further answers wouldn't be forthcoming. "None of your fucking business. So we got a deal or not?"

"Not."

Vicky could only watch in disbelief—and, yes, amazement—as Gene refused the deal in a very final fashion. In a blur of motion, his gun hand rose, and he fired. With a single bullet, he hit the guy who'd offered the ultimatum. As Vicky watched, he fell in slow motion to the ground. Dead.

Ohmygodhekilledhim.

Wide-eyed bravery be damned. She let darkness swallow her.

Chapter Thirteen

It didn't take eyes in the back of his head to know Vicky watched. Vicky feared. Oh, and judging by the thump he heard, Vicky passed out. Good, it would make what Gene had to do next a little less traumatizing. To her at any rate.

With long strides, unhurried but not masked in any way, he approached the second snowmobile, his gun held at the ready. He needn't have bothered. The second shooter and driver was in no shape to fight back. The human lay on the ground, one leg pinned under his snowmobile, his blood staining the snow as he whimpered.

"Please don't kill me. Please don't kill me."

"Says the asshole who just seconds ago was shooting at an unarmed woman."

"I didn't want to. I was just doing my job," he blubbered.

As if Gene cared. *This asshole was shooting at my Pima.* Apparently, it was something on the do-not-do list or you'll piss off my bear. It was all Gene could do to stop his polar side from surfacing and tearing the fucker to shreds.

Killing the human, while momentarily satisfying, wouldn't solve anything. Gene needed answers.

"What job?"

"I don't know nothing. I wasn't the one in charge."

Wrong answer.

With a nonchalance he felt and didn't have to feign, Gene leaned on the snowmobile, crushing the guy's leg.

Once the human was done screaming, he asked again. "What job?"

Blubbering, the thug replied, "The job to kill the girl."

Kill Vicky? But why? His Pima wouldn't harm a fly, so he couldn't see it as revenge. And why the elaborate scheming? "Where did you get this job? And from who?"

"I don't know the exact details."

He leaned and checked on the ammo left in his gun, reloading it with the bullets he found in the pocket while the idiot screamed.

After a few seconds he eased the pressure and waited for the idiot to talk.

"Randy was the one in charge. He's the one who spotted the hit."

"Spotted it where?"

"Online on a forum."

"You mean you got a contract to kill Vicky off the fucking Internet?" Gene couldn't help his incredulity.

"Of course. It's how it's all done nowadays." Even in pain, the guy had the nerve to sound cocky.

"I know how it's done." He just didn't understand the target. "How much was the job for?"

"Five hundred."

"Dollars?"

"Thousand."

Gene couldn't help but whistle. Whoever wanted Vicky dead wasn't playing around. Which meant there'd be other attempts. But it still didn't explain the why. "Any idea why her death is so important?"

"Like I said, I wasn't in on the deal. Randy just offered me some bucks if I helped. We was supposed to make it look like an accident."

"So you were the ones who drugged her coffee?"

"We hoped she'd drink some and fall asleep when she went exploring."

Where the low temperatures would make it look like she froze to death. "How were you supposed to collect?"

"Once her death was confirmed, Randy was supposed to call a number."

A number Gene would wager led to a disposable phone with no way of tracing the owner. "What's this forum's name where the job was posted?"

"You pay them we slay them dot com."

How tacky.

"Got anything else to say?"

"Nothing. I swear. This was just supposed to be an easy hit. Follow her to this fucking forsaken place. Make sure she had an accident and collect."

"And then I came along and fucked things up." Gene smiled.

The idiot smiled back. "Exactly. Nothing personal. Just business."

His Pima was more than just business, and, yes, it was fucking personal. Gene aimed his weapon and the guy suddenly realized he looked death in the eye.

"Mercy, man. Please. I promise to not come after her anymore."

"No you won't." Because Gene wasn't one to leave loose ends. Nor did he show mercy. It wasn't the villain way.

The gunshot echoed, but at least by shooting, he kept blood off his hands. He did so hate having to explain the stains when he went into town.

And to town they'd have to go if he wanted more answers.

Even though he'd eliminated this set of killers, Gene couldn't return Vicky to the camp, not without knowing if more of them hid in plain sight waiting for their chance to net half a mill. He also couldn't just stick her on a plane for home, wherever that might be. If these idiots were willing to brave the arctic for cash, then Pima wouldn't stand a chance in the city. Not with that kind of payout up for grabs.

Five hundred K. A staggering amount for anyone, but not a temptation to Gene. Gene didn't kill for money. When he took a life, it was to benefit one person only. Him. Him and his vengeance. Him and his need for violence. And now his need to protect.

Blech. Damned woman was proving more and more troublesome. A smart bear would dump her unconscious ass now and go his merry way. However, Gene needed only one look at her sleeping features, with her luscious lips slightly parted, her glasses askew to know he couldn't abandon her.

She'd die without his help, and for some reason, that bothered him.

Oh please don't tell me I'm growing a conscience. He'd thought himself rid of that along with his morals, but apparently like a tenacious weed, it was trying to grow back.

He'd allow it, for now, but if it got in his way, watch out, because he would shed blood if he needed to rid himself of anything that might make him weak.

Even a cute little human.

Okay, maybe not his Pima, but only because there was no honor or challenge in killing a woman.

However, if he wasn't dumping or killing her, what was his next move?

I need to see what's happening in this so-called forum that's contracting hits and get to the bottom of who wants her dead. Then Gene could do what he did best. Kill something.

He straddled the snowmobile and gunned it. Next stop, a little town on the Alaskan border where he kept another stash in a hidey-hole. Once there, he could decide his next move.

Chapter Fourteen

The icy plain stretched in a never-ending white sheet. Nowhere to hide. No succor in sight. Nothing to protect her from the polar bear chasing her.

Chest heaving, legs burning, and fear keeping her upright, Vicky ran as fast as she could, knowing that if she stopped, the bear would get her.

She made a mistake. One almost every person being chased makes. She peered over her shoulder to gauge how far behind her the beast was.

Not far enough. Her curiosity cost her.

It shouldn't have surprised her when her feet tangled and she fell forward. At least she knew well enough by now to thrust her hands in front of her to absorb most of the impact, instead of letting her face bear the brunt. However, an unblemished visage wouldn't help her given she'd lost any lead or chance of escaping the deadly predator intent on having her.

Rolling to her back, she couldn't help but scrabble backward, panting in fright as the massive polar bear, with the vivid blue gaze, lumbered toward her.

His muzzle pulled back in a snarl.

His gaze, cold and hungry.

She shut her eyes and whimpered, praying for sweet oblivion so she wouldn't have to meet her demise. *Why can't I faint?* Now of all times the skill failed her.

Eyes shut tight, she didn't see the bear catch up to her, but she could swear she felt its shadow cover her. Despite her terror, she couldn't help but peek, and then gasp.

The slavering maw of a polar bear wasn't what she saw but the cynical gaze of a man. A naked man.

"Gene?"

"You expected someone else?"

"But the bear...Where did he go?"

"Nowhere."

And with those puzzling words, he lowered his head and—

Thump. Vicky roused to the lulling rumble of a snowmobile and a knock to the head as she hit the side of the sled. *Ouch.* She took a moment to blink in the darkness, a pitch-black unrelieved by even the twinkle of a single star.

I'm alive. But in whose hands she couldn't tell with the blanket draping her head. Given the kind gesture, though, meant to keep her from frostbite, she could guess.

Gene. A guess confirmed with a quick glance. No mistaking his broad back or the odd tingling awareness she got when around him.

He'd prevailed over the attackers, once again her hero, even if a reluctant one.

She stayed nestled in her cocoon, not ready to move yet, not with her mind trying to come to grips with the fact the killers weren't after Gene. *They were after me!*

Someone wanted her dead. *Me. Victoria Lola Sanchez, who never had an enemy in my life, unless you count*

Wendi in the third grade because I spilled my grape juice on her new dress. Other than some inadvertent clumsy accidents, Vicky had never done anything to merit someone wanting to kill her. So she had to ask again, why?

It didn't take her long to guess, thanks to Rick. Dear departed Rick who'd said on more than one drunken occasion the only reason he'd married her fat, boring ass was because she was loaded.

Someone wants my money. Great. Greed probably served as the motivation, but greed on whose part? An only child, an orphan since her late teens, and a widow, who would benefit if she died?

I don't even have an updated will. The last one she had notarized left everything to Rick. What would happen to her assets if she were to die now? Did Rick have some kind of distant cousin who thought he'd inherit? Did she have some until now unknown family member just waiting to get their hands on her inheritance?

"I know you're awake," Gene said out of the blue, his voice loud enough to carry even over the rumble of the snowmobile.

"No, I'm not," she replied, intentionally this time, with a smile he couldn't see.

"How are you feeling?"

Good question. She sat up and took stock. Other than a stiffness in her joints from lying in the sledge, "Pretty good. Just a bit sore."

"I'll stop in a bit so we can eat and stuff."

And stuff being an uncomfortable squat in the snow to pee while he stood guard. Cheeks burning, she kicked snow as best as she could over it, which for some reason amused him.

"Hiding it doesn't mean I don't know it's there," he remarked.

"A gentleman wouldn't mention it."

It didn't take his leer to guess his next words. "I'm not a gentleman, Pima."

No, he certainly wasn't. Nor a shining example of a hero with his foul language. Certainly not a valorous knight with his habit of killing people. And yet, Vicky couldn't help but trust and like him, despite his flaws. Beneath the irritable loner hid a good man, one who wouldn't let her come to harm, who put his life on the line for her.

Oh my god, I'm like a cliché. Chubby nerd girl falls for violent bad boy.

How exciting.

"What's got you grinning?" he grumbled, having caught her mid fantasy.

"Uh. Well. I was just thinking—"

"Sounds dangerous."

She blinked in surprise. Had Gene actually made a jest? "I was thinking, that um, maybe we should camp for a few hours, you know so you can get some sleep. You must be tired."

"Why, Pima, are you trying to get me in the sack?"

Her cheeks could have boiled water with the heat infusing them. "No. Of course not." Although the thought might have crossed her mind. But how could he have guessed that?

A short laugh barked forth from him as he caught sight of her in the glare of the snowmobile headlights. "Holy shit, you're blushing."

"Am not," she mumbled.

"Liar," he chided.

"It was just a suggestion. Sorry I made it."

"Actually, I think stopping is a good idea. This stretch between here and the border to Alaska can prove treacherous. I'd rather navigate it by daylight in case we run into trouble."

"You think there might be more of those guys still after us?"

"Yes."

She gasped.

"Not out here though," he added with a naughty grin.

Oh how she almost melted. Funny how a mischievous smile could transform his craggy features and render him even more attractive than before.

I've got it so bad. What a shame nothing would ever come of it. Gene had made it very clear he thought she was a pain in his buttocks. His Pima. Although, of late, he seemed to say it with less disparagement than before.

"If you're not worried about an attack, then what are you worried about?"

"The kind of trouble I'm talking about is fissures and drifts, the kind that could cause serious damage to our sled. I don't know about you, but I'd prefer not to walk a few hundred miles to the closest town."

Hundreds? A number that brought home just how remote they truly were. Why, a man could do anything to her out here and no one would ever know—or hear. "Do we have what we need to camp?" she managed to squeak in spite of her rapidly beating heart.

"Let's find out."

When it came to surviving, Gene knew his stuff. In short order, he'd fabricated some kind of shelter using a tarp and the side of the sledge. Inside this low-angled lean-to, he placed a pair of sleeping bags, unzipped from their singular state and rezipped together to form one large cocoon.

She eyed the makeshift bed with trepidation and, yes, some excitement. "We're sharing?"

"I don't want either of us freezing to death. Just do me a favor and kick off your boots before climbing in. Oh and shed the coat. With the pair of us in that sucker, things will stay hot enough."

With an unseemly haste, Vicky obeyed and crawled into the low-ceilinged tent. In moments, a big body had joined her, making the ample space tight. So tight that her body ended up pressed against his.

Gene groaned.

"Are you okay?" she asked anxiously, unable to see his face in the dark. "Did I poke you somewhere?"

"I'm fine," he growled.

"Oh." She lay on her side, facing away from him but aware of how her buttocks pressed against his thighs. She couldn't help but shiver, awareness of him doing strange things to her body.

"You're cold." He stated, didn't ask, as Gene went from lying on his back to his side. To her surprise, his arm curled around her waist and drew her into him.

She almost gasped in surprise, the intimacy shockingly pleasant. Her head ended up tucked under his chin, her back against his chest, her rear nestled against his groin. Oh my. Even she knew what the hardness pressing against her meant.

I'm arousing him.

For some reason this elated her. She tried to ignore a nagging voice, that sounded remarkably like Rick's, insisting that Gene, like any normal, hot-blooded male who'd gone without sex for a while, would have the same reaction if put in close proximity with a woman. Really, given his rough handsomeness and killer body, he could do much better than a chubby geek like her. He could—

"What's got your mind whirling a mile a minute?" he asked. Gone was his usual sarcastic tone. He sounded almost gentle, as if their intimate pose in the darkness was a hideaway where he didn't need to put on a brash front.

Thank goodness he couldn't see her cheeks now. He'd guess for sure. As to admitting aloud her thoughts? Never. With her luck he'd laugh at her. Or, worse, pity her.

"Nothing, just wondering about everything that's happened." Which wasn't entirely untrue.

"Do you have any idea who might want you dead?" he asked.

She shook her head. "No. The only thing I can think of is someone is after my money."

"You rich?"

Again she nodded.

"Who stands to inherit?"

"That's just it, nobody. I have no close family, and Rick's dead. I don't know who would benefit from me dying."

"Maybe it's for vengeance."

"For what? I haven't hurt anyone."

"Are you sure? Maybe some guy's jealous girlfriend or wife isn't happy you slept with their significant other."

She couldn't help her laughter. "You think someone would be jealous of *me*?" A note of incredulity colored her reply. "That's ridiculous."

"I don't see the humor. You're very attractive."

This time she snorted. "How long have you been out here? I am nothing close to the modern definition of gorgeous. Cute maybe if you're into chubby geeks, but I can assure you, that's not the case. Besides, I haven't had a date since Rick died. As a matter of fact, I've never been with anyone else." Why she admitted that sad fact she couldn't have said, but now that she'd admitted the pitiful truth, she couldn't take it back.

"You've only been with the one man?"

She nodded. "I know it's pathetic."

"That's not the word I would have used," he mumbled in a low voice.

"Well, it's the reality, which is why I doubt jealousy is the reason behind the attacks. Are you absolutely certain they weren't after you?"

"Why, Pima, are you trying to shift the blame to me for the murderous attempts on your life? Are you implying I'm the type of guy to have enemies?"

She squirmed, and she could have sworn he growled. His grip around her waist certainly got tenser. "You're the one who said he had people out to hurt him."

Gene chuckled. "Indeed, I did. And I do. But alas, in this case, it seems it is not I who is the target but you, my *luscious* Pima."

How huskily he said it, the word almost a caress. She couldn't help but flush with heat, and awareness tingled within her, urging her to do something more than just lie in his embrace. But to do anything else was too forward. Never mind the bravery she'd shown when she'd given him the one kiss, alone, in the dark with no distraction or escape, no way could she act on the urges heating her body.

"What do we do next?"

"I can think of a few things," he murmured, the palm of his hand flattening against her belly, and his face nuzzling her hair.

"Like?" She whispered the word.

"The right answer is to keep moving until we reach a town and I can get a hold of some contacts and truly see what's going on with you."

"And the wrong answer?" She held her breath, both wanting and fearing the reply.

"Don't tempt me, or I'll show you," he growled, his hand pulling her tight against him where his erection pressed hard and insistent against her.

"What if I want you to show me?" she asked, the intimate moment giving her a bravery she never possessed in daylight.

He didn't reply. Instead, his whole body shuddered, and he buried his face in the vee where her shoulder and neck met. His teeth gripped the skin there, a sharp tug. She gasped.

"You don't know what you're asking."

The darkness and his words gave her the courage to act. When else would she ever have the chance? She turned until she faced him, unable to see him in the pitch-black but feeling his warm breath, and even better, when she placed her hands against his chest, she felt the rapid thump of his racing heart.

"I've never had anyone make me feel like this before," she admitted.

"I can't give you what you need."

And what do you think I need?"

"A relationship. A home. A life without chaos."

"I'm not asking for those. I just want to feel close to someone."

"And you're choosing me?" An incredulous note crept into his reply.

"I know it's crazy. I barely know you, and we're such opposites, but…" She trailed off, suddenly hesitant about revealing so much to him.

"But?" he queried softly.

She let out a soft sigh. "When I'm around you, you make me feel alive. And safe. You make me want…" She swallowed. "You."

Chapter Fifteen

I want you.

The words almost brought a roar to his lips. How dare she do that to him? Seduce him first with her presence, then her admitted innocence, and, now, with her blatant desire.

He could tell she didn't lie. He could smell her arousal. Feel her need. A need reciprocated.

Perhaps had they shared this conversation in daylight and several feet apart instead of cocooned together in the darkness, the space so intimate, so private, he might have stood a chance. Perhaps, he could have fought her allure.

Doubtful.

Even his bear thought he was fooling himself. From the first moment he'd met Vicky, he'd fought his attraction to her. To hear her disparage herself, to know she didn't see her outer beauty, which matched an inner goodness, made him want to shake her. And kiss her. And worship every inch of her until she grasped just how lovely and tempting she truly was.

But he held back. He was so wrong for her. A goodness like hers should never bear his taint. Yet, what could he do when she practically begged him? When she so sweetly asked him to make her feel alive, to satisfy her needs?

Right here, right now, with only the two of them, he was just a man and she a woman. Both needing the same thing. Both wanting each other.

A man only had so much restraint.

And she crushed it.

The soft press of her lips against his, hesitant and unsure, cemented his fate.

Right or wrong, he had to give her something and, in return, perhaps keep a little something for himself, capture a little of her innocence to remind him the world wasn't all bad.

He cupped her head, the silky strands of her hair soft against his calloused palm. Her lips parted as he nibbled on her lower one, her sweet, soft gasp captured by his mouth. He breathed her in. Tasted her. Melded with her, his entire focus on pleasing this lovely creature who refused to run away.

While at first cautious in her actions, under his persistent caresses, she grew pliant then, hesitantly, demanding. Her hands reached to grip his shoulders, and she squirmed against him, her lower body aroused and seeking what it instinctively knew he could give.

His free hand cradled her close to him, palming her lush buttocks, the fabric of her trousers layered over long johns not able to hide her sweet curves. The tight confines of the sleeping bag made it impossible for him to truly strip and cover her body with his own as he longed to.

But that didn't mean he couldn't touch. Besides, the almost forbidden aspect of gliding his hand under her garments, feeling his way instead of seeing, added an erotic element. Her breath caught as his hand caressed the smooth skin of her lower back. He could have groaned at the way she trembled when his hand skimmed to the front, gliding upward along her rib cage until he reached the swell of her breast.

Given their rapid flight and how she'd just piled clothes atop her long johns, she'd not had a chance to fetter them in a bra. Bonus for him.

With nothing in his way, he cupped the full globe, more than a handful and, judging by the thumb that brushed over the peak, possessed of fat nipples.

He growled, wishing they were in a real bed where he could strip her and latch onto it. Nibble and suck. But he couldn't, which in itself was a form of erotic torture that only served to enflame him.

Lucky for him, she quite enjoyed his stroke and pinch of her nipple. She shivered and mewled, her lips hot and panting as they remained locked in a sensual embrace that involved a lot of tongue.

His Pima learned quickly, her first hesitant forays against his tongue now sensual thrusts that he fully savored.

When he was done teasing her taut nipples, he let his hand travel again, down and down some more, until he reached the waistband of her bottoms.

He stopped, and she tensed, breath held. Teasingly, he didn't immediately penetrate the fabric but instead stroked over it, cupping her mound and sensing her heat, imagining the moisture pooling.

It was enough to make him drool. Once again, he wished them anywhere but here because he would have dearly loved to rip the garments from her lower half and bury his face between her thighs, lapping the sweet honey he knew he'd find there.

He pressed hard against the seam of her pants, right against her sex.

She gasped his name. "Gene."

Had anyone ever said his name with such softness and longing?

It made him more determined than ever to bring her pleasure. To have her say his name again, but this time when she came.

I want her to scream my name. Mine.

Impatient now, a man with a mission, he invaded the pants that dared stand between him and his treasure. He raked his fingers through the curls covering her mound, kept going until he hit moisture. Hot. Silky. Wet.

Holy fuck. She was more than ready for him. Just a gentle glide of his finger across her damp nether lips had her shaking against him.

Her cries came more rapidly, more frantic as he simply rubbed back and forth, wetting his fingers before dipping into her oh-so-tight and ready channel.

Her body went rigid. Surely she wasn't— She was. A mini orgasm had her sex clenching tight, and Gene's cock could have burst it was so ready to join her.

But he wanted more than just a small pleasure for her. He wanted her screaming so he kept dipping his finger in and out, adding a second finger to stretch her. It was when he added the stroke to her clit, her swollen bud slick with her juices, that finally his passionate Pima unleashed.

"Gene." She moaned his name as she clutched at him. "Gene. Gene. Gene." She chanted his name in time to the thrust of his fingers and stroke of her clit.

Faster he stroked. Deeper. Harder. His hips arched in time to the cadence, desperately wishing it was his cock buried to the hilt in her moist sex.

He began to murmur to her, something he'd never done before but, in this place and time, seemed right. "Come for me, Vicky. Let yourself go and cream me. Scream for me. Let me feel and hear your pleasure."

"Oh god," she mumbled just before her body tensed. "Oh god…Gene!"

There it was, the glory-filled moment he'd worked for. The cry that was both his name and a praise as she climaxed. And climaxed hard.

The muscles of her sex gripped his fingers so tight he feared moving them. But he did enjoy the ripple of her climax enough that he almost came himself.

Holding her close, his kiss softening to simple brushes across her swollen lips, he cradled her close, a moment so foreign and intimate. Yet right.

Oh fuck, how could it feel so right? So perfect? He still throbbed with need. His cock ached to come, and yet, he'd never felt so satisfied in his life.

How is that possible? And why did a part of him never want the moment to end?

This couldn't last. Not just the moment but his time with her. Once he got her to safety, they would have to part ways. Their future paths didn't lie together.

He had vengeance to plot, and she…she deserved better than him.

The bear within chuffed in pride as his timid little Pima fell asleep against him. Trusting him. *Me!* The worst predator around. The vilest enemy a person could ask for. The biggest fucking teddy bear where she was concerned.

Sigh.

So much for his reputation as a badass. But only if people found out. And he could always kill anyone who mocked him. That would shut them up.

Chapter Sixteen

"Get your ass moving, Pima. The sun has risen, and it's time we made some tracks."

Stretching in the sleeping bag, alone because Gene had somehow managed to exit it without waking her, she didn't immediately reply. She couldn't because memories of the previous night rushed in to greet her.

Oh my god, I can't believe we made out like that. More than made out. Gene made her climax and, boy, did that pleasure eclipse her previous experiences with Rick. To think, Gene did it with only kisses and his hand, which in retrospect embarrassed her.

How sad that it took so little to bring her to orgasm. He must think her so pathetic and unappreciative. Here he'd given her fantastic pleasure, and what had she done for him in return? Fallen asleep.

Some thank you.

Worse than that, though, how to face him? There was no pure darkness to shield her. No pretending the previous night didn't happen. How would he treat her? How should she act?

A vivid streak of dawning sunlight hit her as he unpinned the tarp and whipped it back. She squinted her eyes shut with a squeaked, "Ack! Bright light."

"Yes, my sleeping vampire. Bright light, as in daylight, as in get moving. We've got lots of ground to cover."

So much for the soft lover she'd met the night before. Welcome back, grumpy bear.

With those words, he turned and tromped away while she struggled to emerge from the sleeping bag and slip on her coat and boots without getting all snowy. Well, at least she didn't have to worry about how to act.

Gene seemed back to his usual ornery self. The gentle side she'd met in the darkness had washed away with the daylight. It almost made her wonder if she'd imagined it, yet, her sticky thighs and the still-swollen plumpness of her lower parts all pointed to it having happened.

Dressed, she folded the sleeping bag as Gene puttered around filling the snowmobile gas tank from the spare jerry can strapped to the back of the sledge.

Lucky for them, none of the flying bullets the night before had struck it. She couldn't imagine having to walk. Everywhere she looked, she could see only miles and miles of unrelieved icy, white wasteland.

Out of the blue she asked, "Why did you choose to live here?"

At first she thought he wouldn't reply. "It's quiet."

"But don't you get lonely?" Even Vicky, who couldn't boast many friends, another thing Rick discouraged, found it a little too barren for her taste.

"I have no need of friends."

That wasn't what she'd asked. She frowned and persisted. "Why not?"

"Because."

"But—"

He turned with a snarled, "What is this? Twenty fucking questions?"

Taken aback, she recoiled. "I'm sorry, I was just curious about you."

"Curious?" He barked a disparaging sound. "Fine. You want to know why I choose to live out here, on my fucking own? I'll tell you why. Because I'm an asshole. Because I hate people. You can't trust anyone. Not even your so-called friends."

Who had hurt Gene to make him feel so vehemently? She found herself saying, "I wouldn't betray you."

He sneered. "Words. Meaningless words. I've heard those before. You say you wouldn't betray me now, but when it becomes a life or death situation, you'll think differently. Just like my good ol' pals, you'll walk away and not look back."

"That seems a little harsh."

"Welcome to my world, Pima."

His expression and mini rant should have clamped her lips tight. She knew, were this Rick, she would have never dared. But Gene, while loud and volatile, wouldn't hurt her for asking questions. Of this she was certain. Or was about to find out. "If you hate everyone so much, then why are you helping me?"

"I've been asking myself that very same question."

So much for a sudden romantic declaration. While Vicky hadn't truly expected him to admit undying love at first sight, she'd expected something a little more and couldn't help disappointment. "I will pay you back."

He whirled on her with eyes blazing. "I'm not doing this for fucking money."

"Then why are you?"

He turned away to fiddle with the snowmobile and didn't answer.

But she wanted to know. "Why are you helping me?" *Say it's because you care.* How she wanted to hear him admit it.

"Why? I'd say that's obvious. Because if I don't, you'll die."

"And yet, according to you, you don't care about anybody, so why do you care if someone kills me?" A rare determination saw her accusing him, her hurt over his seemingly casual dismissal of the intimacy they shared fueling her courage. That and an implicit belief that, no matter what she said, he wouldn't retaliate. Not with fists at any rate, but funny how words could hurt more.

"I don't know why!" he roared, finally facing her, his face twisted and angry, yet at the same time anguished as if he fought an inner war. "You're weak. And innocent. And everything I'm not. I should leave you to your fate. Yet for some damnable reason, I can't walk the fuck away. If I could, I would. I have better things to do than protect your fainting little ass."

For some reason she couldn't stop herself from asking, "Like?"

"I don't know. Plotting vengeance. Seal hunting. Getting drunk. Or laid."

She recoiled at his last rebuke. "I'm sorry about last night. I guess I was selfish."

He scrubbed a hand over his face. "Fuck. That's not what I meant. Last night was a mistake, but not because of anything you did. Trust me when I say you did everything right. The problem was, I should have never let things go that far. Now you're expecting things from me. Things I can't give you."

Funny because she didn't recall making any demands. "Like what?"

"I'm not talking about this, Pima. What happened last night was a momentary lapse of sanity. You needed comfort, I gave it to you."

If he called that comfort…

"It won't happen again."

She couldn't help but say, "Ever?"

"Ever." And with that final declaration, he cranked the snowmobile, the rumble of the motor filling in the void between them. "Get in the sled."

"And if I refuse?"

He eyed her, and she bit her lip. *I think I've pushed him enough.* Courage to question was all well and good, but her newfound courage where he was concerned didn't give her the right to badger him. Gene obviously had some deep-seated issues, especially when it came to trusting, and commitment.

With the tarp neatly folded and the sleeping bags rolled and strapped in at her back, Vicky clambered into the sledge, trying to figure out where she'd gone wrong. Last night, he'd seemed so different. Today? For some reason she couldn't grasp, Gene appeared angry with her and himself.

Probably because I threw myself at him like a hussy.

Yet, he'd seemed amenable at the time. She'd not imagined his erection, or his enjoyment. So why the cruel words today? Why the attempt to erect a barrier between them?

Is it because he truly doesn't care, or is it something deeper? Gene was obviously a man troubled by his past. Why else would a man with obvious intelligence and skill hide out here in the middle of nowhere? Gene had secrets. Gene had enemies. Gene had serious issues. Gene was acting like a jerk.

So why did she find herself more attracted to him than ever? Hadn't she experienced enough abuse at the hands of her father and then her husband?

Did a part of her crave a male in her life whom she could never please and who felt a need to berate her?

I thought I promised myself to never allow anybody that kind of power again. Yet here I am. First attractive man who pays me more than a moment of attention and I'm falling right back into that trap.

No. She couldn't allow it. She'd spent years miserable because of one abusive husband. She wouldn't get caught in another relationship where she was treated less than a person and where the respect was lacking.

No matter how sexy, or drawn to Gene she was, she'd have to keep her distance. It didn't prove hard, not with the wall Gene erected between them.

Chapter Seventeen

For the first time in years, the asshole routine didn't sit well with Gene and yet, what choice did he have?

When he'd woken with Vicky nestled in his arms, the scent of her surrounding them, on his fingers, in his blood, even in his damned soul, he'd freaked. Freaked because his first impulse was to kiss her awake and pleasure her again. And again. And…

Keep her. Keep her as mine. Forever.

Panic attack!

It didn't matter that he reminded himself bad guys didn't get to keep good girls. His bear scoffed at the idea they couldn't stay together because they were so different. Opposites were supposed to attract. The strong should pair with the weak. A bear could have his human—and eat her too.

Still though, him and a woman, in a relationship?

A part of him was tempted to try. He wanted to try and see if he could live a normal life, with her. In the real world. Which meant forgetting his plans for vengeance.

But if I'm not plotting revenge, then what else would I do?

I could try my hand at real life again. Get a job. Settle down. Settle down with my Pima.

A fucking farfetched fantasy.

Not only did he doubt his ability to turn himself into a pansy-assed yuppie for Vicky, he doubted very much *he* would ever let him live long enough to enjoy it. One day *he* would find Gene and make him pay. Worse, if *he* suspected Gene had fallen for a human, her life would be in worse danger than it was currently.

The torture, pain, and fear his newest sworn enemy would inflict on his sweet, innocent Pima…Gene couldn't, make that wouldn't, allow her to come to any harm, which meant distancing himself, here and now. No more tasting those lips. No thrusting his fingers into her sex as she cried his name. Nothing. Zilch. Nada.

Grumble.

His inner bear did not like his decision. At all.

Too bad. I'm the one in charge. And I say getting involved is a bad idea.

Grrrr.

Don't you growl at me. It's for the best. We have to do this to keep her safe.

Safe? Apparently his inner bear scoffed at this excuse, as it sent him an image of a snow goose flapping its wings and running around in circles.

Are you calling me bird-brained?

He didn't need to hear the chuffing to know his bear laughed at him. Gene ignored the taunts of his other half. He knew what he had to do. Like it or not.

With his plan determined, he woke Vicky from her peaceful slumber and almost gave in at her first shy good morning smile.

Only by acting as an asshole, which for once didn't come easily, could he stop himself from kissing away the hurt he saw in her eyes.

He did this for her own good.

In stilted silence—his bear sulking in a corner of his mind and her nursing a wounded ego—they traveled, miles and miles, stopping only for essentials like bathroom breaks and refueling from increasingly light gas cans. They were practically running on fumes when he finally hit an outpost that could refuel him. It couldn't have happened at a better time as night was descending with its icy fingers. They spent the night on the floor of the store, Vicky's credit card, which she'd smartly packed, paying not only for the fuel but their warm, if less than comfortable, accommodations.

The sleeping bags were laid out in front of the pellet stove, with some of their gear tucked between them, a barrier to intimacy, which she couldn't fail to note but didn't remark on. Surely he wasn't disappointed that she didn't protest?

The braver version of Vicky, who'd only just begun to blossom, retreated, once more hidden beneath a shy veneer. It pissed him off, but he didn't know how to fix it. Screaming at her probably wouldn't work. It drove him mental when she flinched, especially since he'd never hurt her. At least physically, however it wasn't just fists that could damage. He well knew the power of words.

What a pity he couldn't drag her into his arms and kiss her until she realized his anger was just an act. How he wanted to.

Blue balls weren't comfortable, and neither was a constant erection. Yet to satisfy his needs would break the promise he'd made to himself about staying away.

All he could do was put up with it. Clench his teeth as she once again hesitated when she spoke. Tighten his jaw when she wouldn't meet his eyes. Suppress a growl as she kept quiet. Too quiet.

He hated it, but he'd hate himself more if he or his enemies hurt her. So despite the fact he'd squashed her spirited nature when around him, he maintained his aloof stance.

They traveled like this for a few days until they reached Alaska and the first decent-sized town they'd encountered thus far, if a town of a few hundred could be called sizable. Populated mostly with humans and a small clan of mixed shifters, this tiny pocket of civilization was also where he kept another hidey-hole. Not much really, a room above a bar that he'd paid for in cash to the owner, whom he'd encountered during his army days. Yet another shifter who knew how to keep his mouth shut and not ask questions.

Behind the closed door, which the floss he'd tied off and was still intact showed as undisturbed, the first problem presented itself. The room measured less than a hundred square feet, which meant he couldn't avoid her; smelling her, sensing her, desiring. It didn't help it was just the two of them, some weapons and supplies—oh and a mattress on the floor that kept taunting him.

As Vicky used the small lavatory across the hall, her lips curving in the first smile he'd seen in days at the mention of a shower, he tried not to think of her. It didn't work, not when he knew she was washing her curvy body, soaping it, touching it…

Gene closed his eyes but couldn't stop himself from fantasizing even more. Vicky exiting the shower stall, her tanned skin moist and fresh from the water. Dewy and in need of a lick. His lick. His touch.

He knew he could seduce her. Quiet didn't mean she'd lost her desire for him. On the contrary, as soon as she returned from her bathing—fully dressed in clean clothes and not a flimsy towel, dammit—he could smell her arousal. *Her need, for me.*

It threatened to drive him insane. Almost made him snap and take what he needed.

Take…

Oh fuck. He chose to escape, with a gruff, "Don't let anyone in while I use the facilities."

Fleeing one enclosed space for an even smaller one that she'd just vacated didn't help. Her scent clung to the steam. As he bathed, he couldn't help inhaling it and cursing. Cursing even as he finally sought to relieve the pressure in his cock, his hand smoothly sliding the length of it, eyes closed, too easily imagining her with him. Coming with her name on his lips—dammit—didn't relieve the pressure, or his inexplicable desire for Vicky.

Dressing in the cramped washroom, ears peeled in case of trouble, he pep-talked himself.

No thinking about Vicky. Or looking, or touching.

Concentrate on vengeance. Even if he couldn't muster enthusiasm for it currently.

Devise a plan of action to flush out whoever was behind the attacks on his Pima. *And kill 'em.*

Stay out of *his* reach and make sure she didn't come to *his* attention. Which meant laying low and not making any waves until he'd secured her somewhere safe. Funny how the only safe haven he could think of was with the very men he wanted to take down.

With his head on straighter, he marched back across the hall to his quarters. He walked in, got hit by a wave of awareness—*How sweet she smells*—and instantly his eyes searched her out. Standing by the window, she peered out through the crack in the blinds. She practically jumped out of her skin when he said, "You forgot to lock the door."

"Sorry."

Stop apologizing, he wanted to yell. But that wouldn't help matters. Unlike him, she wasn't used to living on edge, constantly looking over her shoulder and trying to stay one step ahead of enemies. "We'll be staying here for a few days."

No asking why or questioning his decision. She simply nodded. A woman cowed and determined to not raise his ire.

Which pissed him off. He snapped, "Would you stop the whole battered-woman syndrome? I thought we'd clarified the fact I wouldn't hit you."

"I know."

"Then why the beaten look? What happened to the new Pima I met out on the arctic plains looking for adventure?"

She shrugged as she stared at her feet. "Adventure turned out to not be what I expected."

"Meaning?"

"Meaning, maybe it was a bad idea. Maybe I should have never ventured forth from my safe shell and life."

"I never said that."

"You didn't, but you implied it. And you're right. I didn't belong out there in the arctic. I don't belong here. I don't belong anywhere," she finished in a soft whisper.

"That's not what I meant."

"Isn't it?" For a moment, she faced him, her eyes big and lost behind her dark-framed glasses. "I might be afraid of a lot of things, but admitting I was wrong isn't one of them. Silly me, I thought I could reinvent myself. Be strong."

"You can."

A shake of her head sent her damp hair swinging. "Not with you. Not against those guys who attacked me."

"Extenuating circumstances. Besides, I thought we'd already ascertained I was an asshole, which means you shouldn't pay attention to anything I say. As for those hired guns, you did the best you could."

"But if it weren't for my polar bear and you, I'd be dead. And no one would care."

He almost said, *I would*. Because dammit he did care. However, to admit that was to admit he'd lied to her. That he'd purposely acted the jerk to keep her away. He kept his lips clamped shut.

It served only to increase the woebegone expression in her eyes.

Fuck me. Forget the torture by the rebels. She's going to kill me if she actually starts to cry.

A little bit of her former spirit entered her tone as she paced in a tight circle, agitation firing her lagging spirits. "What's the point of trying? You can't protect me forever. We don't even know who's doing this or why."

"We'll find out."

"We?" She laughed, a bitter sound he'd wager she rarely used. "Oh please. I'm sure you're just waiting for a chance to dump me off so you can go back to your life."

What life?

"And I should get back to mine. I guess."

He prodded her. "What happened to adventure?"

"I guess I wasn't cut out for it."

Not true. She'd held up remarkably well given the shit happening to her. He thought fast and tried to find something to remind her of why she'd started her journey. "What about the polar bears? What happened to your whole research thing?"

At this reminder, a ghost of a smile tilted her lips. "I did love the one I got to meet. Even if I didn't manage to collar him with a tracking device."

"Collar him?" Gene couldn't help but sound aghast. "What is it with women trying to shackle free-spirited men?"

"He's a bear, not a man," she reminded with a soft laugh, its sweetness enveloping him and making him yearn for more. "The collar is to track his roaming habits."

"He's a bear. He roams where the food is fresh and his enemies are sparse."

"And what of when he mates?"

"What about it? I'd say that's the bear's business how he does it. He doesn't need anyone watching."

How easily she blushed. "I'm not interested in, um, viewing the act, but more about how he acts. When my polar friend finds a female, will he stick around or leave?"

"He'll never take a mate." Because it would put her in danger.

She arched a brow at his vehemence. "You speak as if you know him."

Very well as a matter of fact. "You could say that. I've crossed paths with him more than a few times."

"Any idea how he got the scar?"

A grimace creased his features as he replied. "Same way I did, by being in the wrong place at the wrong time."

She didn't push him. Good, because some things he preferred not to answer.

"I do wish I'd gotten more pictures of him. He truly was magnificent."

A smile curved Gene's lips as his inner bear preened—vain beast. "I'll make sure to tell him."

She made a face at him. "Don't make fun of me. I know I have a tendency of seeing my bears as more than just animals, but I can't help myself. For a long time now, I've felt closer to animals than most people."

"That's because animals are simple to understand."

"Unlike you." She slapped a hand over mouth a moment too late. The accusation hung in the air between them.

But Gene didn't take affront. Instead, an odd yearning twisted his heart, and it made him admit something he never meant to. "A part of me wishes things could be different. That I could be the man you deserve."

"And what kind of man do you think I deserve?"

"An honorable one."

She took a step closer to him and another, which in the tiny space brought her to within inches of him. Angling her chin, she gazed up at him, her eyes big behind her glasses, her expression serious. "But that's just it, Gene. You are the most honorable man I've ever met. The only one to ever treat me like someone of worth."

"If you only knew the things I've done."

"I don't care about your past. I'm judging you on the now. On how you've treated me. Since the moment we've met, you've done nothing but take care of me."

Because he couldn't help himself. "Someone had to," was his gruff reply.

"But that someone didn't have to be you. A lot of people would have left me to my fate. Walked away. It's the easy thing to do. But you didn't. You stuck around. You made sure I was safe, and when I needed you, you came. You saved me."

He couldn't help but whisper, "I'll always keep you safe." So much for his big macho act and his I-don't-give-a-shit-about-anyone speech. With one sentence he'd given her all the evidence she needed to take him down, to smash the walls and lies he'd built to keep her away.

Yet, his admission didn't give her the triumphant expression he expected. She didn't crow in victory. But she did take advantage of his one weakness. His Achilles' heel. His Kryptonite. She fought him with the one weapon destined to destroy him.

Her.

Gene should have pulled away, run, escaped, pulled his gun and shot her before she…

Kissed him.

He was defenseless against her sweet embrace. Frozen prey in the headlight of her trust.

He couldn't move, just feel, and enjoy, as she used her guileless trust against him.

I want her. I need her. I must have her. I—

Needed to escape before he succumbed completely to her allure.

From the tiny room—with the bed that called him and the woman that disarmed him—he fled. Fled with his lips tingling, his arousal raging, and his bear roaring at him to go back.

He'd no sooner slammed the door shut behind him that he heard, "You!"

Addled by the kiss, Gene wasn't working on all cylinders. It was the only excuse he could come up with for not taking his usual precautions. No excuse and he paid for it as a fist came out of nowhere and cracked his head to the side.

Reeling back, he gave his head a half shake and, before even seeing who hit him, snarled, "Fucking asshole. I'll teach you to hit a man out of the blue."

"I dare you to try," snapped a familiar voice.

I'll be damned. Wait, I already am. It seemed Gene had run into another of his old army buddies. Brody, usually a genial person, but rile his wolf—or threaten his clan—and he could turn nasty.

The second swing missed his face as he raised his arm to block it. With a growl of frustration, which had more to do with his blue balls than Brody finding him, Gene charged. He caught the big man around the middle but barely budged him.

The fight, though, was on.

With a flurry of flying fists, they tussled, slamming each other off the walls of the upstairs hall, grappling for the upper hand. The edge of the stairs took them unaware, and in a limb-flailing ball, they tumbled down them, hitting the dusty plank floor of the bar hard. But not hard enough to stop their fight.

Having landed on top, Gene took the opportunity to draw back his fist and drove it into Brody's face.

Brody replied by wedging his knees under his body and flinging him away.

It gave them both the time needed to regain their feet.

"How did you find me?" Gene asked as he eyed his former friend while balancing on the balls of his feet, ready this time for the next swing.

"You might be a ghost when it comes to hiding out, but don't forget, you're not the only one with skills."

"You tracked me?" Surprising given where Gene had spent the last few weeks.

"More like scented."

"I only just arrived."

Brody shrugged. "So I'm lucky. A matter of the right place at the right time. Speaking of time, I think it's time you answered for your actions."

"I don't have time for your clan politics and bullshit."

"Well, then make the time, because I'm not leaving unless I'm dragging your carcass back with me. Dead or alive, that's completely up to you."

"Not going to forgive me like fucking Boris did?" Gene replied with a sneer.

"I might if I thought you could actually change. But given what you've done, I'd say that's highly unlikely. You're a man with a giant fucking tree trunk up his ass, and I, for one, am not going to mollycoddle you yanking it the hell out. Act like an asshole throwing a temper tantrum and you'll get treated like one and get the sound thrashing you deserve."

"I wasn't having a temper tantrum. I was avenging myself," was Gene's indignant reply.

"For what? Being jealous we made it out before you did."

Jealous? "You fucking left me behind!"

"Because we didn't know."

Again with the damned rational answers. Argh. "No excuse." With a roar to shake the rafters, Gene snapped and plowed into Brody. Good-looking, everything-turned-out-fine fucking Brody.

They stumbled together, limbs locked in a hug to the death. Given he was a bear with a slight size advantage over Brody's less stocky wolf build, Gene could have crushed Brody's ribs. He could have ended the fight right then, except for one thing.

The unmistakable sound of a shotgun getting pumped diverted their attention.

The bartender aimed the barrels of a shotgun at them. "Read the fucking sign. No fighting in the bar. Take it outside before I put holes in both your hides."

And he would too. But Gene wasn't ready to stop now, not when he had someone he could finally pummel his frustrations out on. "Shall we rumble some more?" Gene asked with a mocking tilt of his lips and a sweep of his hands toward the door.

"After you," Brody retorted.

Knowing Brody's penchant for a clean fight, Gene led the way, but apparently time had changed his friend just as it had done a number on him. He'd no sooner set foot outside than a boot to the middle of his back sent him stumbling.

He caught himself quickly and whipped around. "Well, well, the wolf now fights dirty."

"Says the man who's been skulking in shadows taking aim at women."

"You know what they say, all's fair in hate and war."

"Real men fight their battles face to face. They don't hide in the darkness toying with innocents. They don't blame others because of their inability to cope."

"Who says I'm not coping?" Gene snapped.

"I wouldn't call blaming us for your treatment by the insurgents coping."

"Funny, because the more I harass you, the better I feel." Lie. He didn't. Gene thought he'd get some satisfaction at hurting those he felt betrayed by. So far, though, it only left him feeling even more hollow than before.

"Let's see how you feel after I beat you to a bloody pulp."

"Bring it, dog." Gene beckoned with his fingers.

With a snarl, Brody came at him. Gene caught his rush and gave him a bear hug in return. However, Brody was no human weakling. He broke the hold and slugged Gene in the gut. Once. Twice.

As they traded blows, Gene became distantly aware they'd gained an audience. Others in the bar, shifters and human alike, having emerged to watch them pummel each other.

Neither combatant truly got the upper hand, evenly matched, especially since both needed to keep their inner beasts leashed. Shifter rule of survival: never let the humans know what you are. His grandmother had taught him that along with the other important one; hiding the wooden spoon didn't stop punishment. It just meant she'd use her cane.

If only his grandma were here now. She'd cheer him on. She always did enjoy a good fight.

Crunch. Brody's already bent nose cracked and angled to the side. Gene had little time to celebrate as a left hook to the side of his head left his ear ringing.

A punch to the teeth split a lip, and blood flowed.

A kick received in the gut whooshed the air from his lungs.

He reacted with a boot of his own, which sent Brody reeling back.

The separation gave them a chance to regroup. Barely breathing hard, Gene couldn't help a smile. "It's been awhile since I've had a good fight."

"Then maybe you should come back with me. I know a few other guys who'd like to take a poke at you."

"If I wasn't on a mission, I might have accepted."

"Ah yes, your mission of vengeance," Brody mocked.

"I see word has gotten around."

"So when were you going to come after me?"

"Feeling left out?" Gene taunted with a stab in his direction.

Brody jumped back. "A little. Why do you think I came to find you?"

"Alas, I wish we had more time to draw this out, but as I said, I've got other shit to take care of before I get to you."

Brody lunged, faked a punch, and spun his leg in a roundhouse that caught Gene in the face. It hurt.

It would leave a great big fucking bruise, but it wasn't enough to take him down.

A pity his Pima didn't know that.

Her horrified gasp cut through the noise of the fight and the jeering audience.

He turned his head to see her staring with big eyes and terror on her face. Before he could reassure her, Brody slugged him, and Gene went down hard, the ground not a forgiving landing spot.

Before he could bounce to his feet, Vicky was there. Standing between him and Brody.

"Don't you hit him," she yelled.

I must be hallucinating. Pima, coming to my defense?

"Or what?" snarled Brody.

"Or—Or—"

Given the way Brody's eyes practically gleamed yellow as his wolf danced behind his orbs, eager to escape, it wasn't any wonder when his delicate Pima began a slow slump to the ground.

Rolling to his knees, Gene caught her before she could hit.

An incredulous appearing Brody stared down at them. "What the fuck is up with her?"

Gene shrugged. "My Pima here doesn't handle stress too well."

"Ya think?"

"It's not her fault," Gene defended. "She had a dick for a husband."

"Had? Did you kill him?"

"I wish," grumbled Gene.

"So who is she?"

In other words, what did she mean to Gene? Given their avid audience, he didn't want to say too much. "Truce while I explain?"

Brody hesitated only a moment before nodding.

Standing with Vicky cradled in his arms, Gene said, "Grab us some beers and meet me in my room."

"Why, so you can shoot me as I come in the door?" Brody accused.

"My word, I won't harm you."

For a moment, Gene wondered if Brody would call his rusty word into question. How long since he'd made a promise to someone, and one he actually intended to keep? Despite his reputation, with a nod, Brody let him walk away. Gene returned to the warmth of the building, his unconscious Pima in his arms.

Or not.

As soon as they hit the stairs, she cracked open an eyelid and whispered, "Are you all right?"

Shocked, he just about dropped her on her head – probably not for the first time in her life.

Chapter Eighteen

The expression on Gene's face when he realized she'd faked her fainting spell?

Awesome. So awesome, she giggled. "If you could see your face right now."

He didn't find it as amusing. "You faked passing out?" he hissed as he took the stairs to their room by two.

"Well, I had to do something. That awful man was hurting you." Never mind the fact that Gene was hurting the stranger back. She'd seen the violence, the savagery, the blood and practically swooned. Until Gene got hit hard when distracted by her arrival. Then she'd gotten mad. Mad enough that she'd acted. *Here I thought he'd be proud.*

"Awful man?" Gene snorted. "Do your glasses need a cleaning? Brody was considered the best-looking guy in our platoon. Women were constantly throwing themselves at him."

The lenses of her glasses were fine. Vicky wrinkled her nose. "I guess he's all right looking." However, he lacked Gene's rugged appeal.

"All right?" he managed to choke out.

She shrugged. "If you like that sort. He's really not my type."

"And what is your type?" Gene asked as he carried her down the hall to their room.

An impish side she never suspected existed said, "He's carrying me right now."

One of his rare smiles tilted his lips. "What am I going to do with you?"

She could think of some things, such as a repeat of the pleasure he'd given her when they were traveling, However, given he'd just invited the guy whom he was fighting up to their room, she doubted they'd have the time. Speaking of whom, "Who was that guy, and why was he attacking you?"

"That guy is an old army buddy of mine."

"Looked more like an enemy," she replied as he deposited her inside their quarters and closed the door.

"He is now. Kind of. It's complicated."

Before she could ask him elucidate, a knock rattled the door. Grabbing the gun that he'd laid earlier within easy reach by his pack, Gene planted himself to one side of the frame while gesturing for her to move over and stay down.

She flattened herself in behind a cardboard box that a quick peek in the open top showed contained freeze-dried ration packs.

Once he seemed satisfied she was out of harm's way, Gene asked, "Who is it?"

"You know goddamn well it's me, Ghost. Let me the fuck in."

"Or what?" Gene asked, an edge of mirth to his query, which baffled her.

Weren't he and this guy just smashing each other? She'd never understand men.

"Or I'll huff and puff and kick your ass to the North Pole and back until you admit I'm your superior."

"Superior? Ha." Gene snorted as he swung open the door and allowed the other man entry.

In strode the buddy/enemy. A tall fellow, broad-shouldered, brown shaggy hair, a bit of a scruffy beard and piercing, almost golden eyes. Now that Gene pointed it out, she supposed he was good looking, if you were into hairy guys with cocky attitudes, but she preferred the clean-cut and rugged handsomeness of her protector.

"You planning on killing me?" Gene asked, his gun down by his side but his posture tense.

"Depends. Are you going to gut me if I blink too long?" asked the hairy stranger.

"I think I can restrain myself."

"Then I guess we're both safe. Has your lady friend recovered?" Given his piercing gaze had already noted her presence, he knew the answer, but Gene replied anyhow.

"She's fine. See for yourself. You can come out, Pima," Gene said without looking in her direction. "Brody won't hurt you."

"Unlike some guys I know," accused Brody with a pointed stare at Gene.

"I never hurt those women," Gene answered.

"Really? Tell that to Tammy. You remember her, don't you? The one you kidnapped and held hostage to draw Reid into a trap. The one, you know,"—Brody shot her a look—"that you *changed*."

At the odd inflection, Vicky frowned and kept frowning as she tried to decipher Brody's accusation. Gene hurt a woman? She couldn't fathom it, and yet Gene didn't defend himself.

"I won't deny I've done some things that crossed some lines."

"Crossed? More like stomped all over. It's a good thing for you it all ended well in that case, and with all the other shit you've caused, or we wouldn't be talking now."

"Not all of Kodiak Point's problems can be laid at my feet. I am not the only one acting against Reid and the rest of you."

"Who is then?" Brody asked as his keen gaze surveyed the room, never straying too long on one item. Much like Gene, he was a man always aware of his surroundings.

"Trust me when I say you're better off not knowing. And don't dig for answers. You might not like the result. Right now, *he's* only got part of his attention on your little corner of the world. Keep quiet and maybe he'll forget you."

"What if we don't want to be forgotten?"

"Then you're dumber than you look. This is not a fight you want to encourage."

Brody sneered. "And I'm supposed to listen to you? A guy allied with this douchebag?"

"Was allied. No longer. You'll be glad to know I am on his shit list. Which is why I need to get Pima's problem dealt with before he finds me and takes me out."

Vicky's eyes widened. She might have only followed part of the conversation, but she didn't have trouble grasping Gene thought he'd die. "Why does he want to kill you?"

Two sets of eyes turned her way, and Vicky clamped her lips tight, suddenly wishing she'd kept quiet.

"Who is she, really?" Brody asked. "Don't tell me Ghost has finally settled down?"

"As if," Gene snorted. "She's just someone I came across who can't seem to stay out of trouble."

Gee, what a warm and fuzzy way of describing their strange relationship. "I'm not doing it on purpose," she mumbled.

"Yet, that hasn't stopped shit from happening to you and around you," Gene rebuked, but not with his usual acerbic tone. "Say hello to Vicky. I met her while she was investigating polar bears in the Arctic Circle."

Brody barked a laugh. "So she kn—"

Gene cut him off. "Knows they are awesome creatures."

"Majestic," she corrected, only to blush as Brody fell against the wall laughing so hard.

"Oh, this is fucking priceless," Brody managed to gasp. "Majestic." This sent him into another gale of laughter while Gene glared.

"I don't see the humor. Polar bears are brave and noble creatures. Much better than say a mangy wolf." It was Gene's turn to smile as Brody sobered and glared back.

"You wish."

"I know."

Vicky wished she could understand the serious miens over which animal was better. She tried to alleviate the tense situation, which, despite the tenseness and the volatile size of the men facing off, for some reason didn't send her into a panic. Despite the testosterone heavy in the air, though, she didn't worry. These men weren't the type to bring her harm.

More and more, she couldn't help but see the difference in how a man could treat her and how much her father and Rick differed—not in a good way. "The polar bears weren't the only incredible thing out there. Gene was probably the most important person I met. He saved me."

Gene shook his head no and made throat cutting gestures.

Catching the motion, Brody stepped in front of Gene and smoothly said, "Really, how? Tell me more?"

"He's saved me quite a few times since we've met. First from the bear and then the poisoned coffee that almost had me freeze to death. Then there were the guys who tried to kill me by making it look like I got attacked by a bear. The bear was the first one to actually save me there, but Gene arrived shortly after."

"And was he by any chance naked?" Brody asked.

A frown creased her forehead. "Yes, how did you know?"

A smile split Brody's lips. "Old Ghost here never did like getting his clothes dirty during battle. And is that all that's happened?"

Having sidestepped Brody to take a sentinel position by the window, Vicky couldn't help but note Gene's resigned expression as Vicky extolled his virtues. "Well, after he found some new clothes, we ended up escaping the camp before the other bad guys could get us. But they started shooting at us. Gene took care of them when they chased us down on snowmobiles, and Gene singlehandedly saved both our lives. Gene's a hero," she finished with a pleased smile in Gene's direction.

Oddly enough, his shoulders were hunched, his head was down, and he shook. Overcome with the trouble she'd caused no doubt.

Turning back to Brody, Vicky couldn't help but note his wide eyes, eyes that got wider the more Vicky rambled on about Gene's general awesome nature.

His incredulity when he snickered, "Ghost, a hero?" was totally uncalled for.

"He is," she insisted, indignant enough to plant her hands on her hips and tilt her chin.

"Are you fucking kidding me?" Brody asked, not of her but Gene.

"I wish. Trust me, I've tried to dissuade her from this foolish fantasy that I'm a decent person, but for some reason, Pima here just won't believe it."

"Because I didn't imagine it. You saved me, which makes you a hero."

"You know, I bet you could carry off those tights. You've got good legs," Brody mused aloud.

"Sounds great especially since I could use them to garrote you," Gene threatened.

"Hey, just trying to help you come up with a proper hero look. You know for when you're called to action."

"Blow me."

"Sorry, bro, but I prefer honey to sausage."

"If you're done mocking me, mind coming back to the business at hand?"

"Business, yeah. Let's start with yours. You need to help Vicky out because you think someone is trying to kill her? Is it your supposed ally turned enemy?"

Gene shook his head and then proceeded to relate, in a little more detail—while omitting certain intimate parts—the series of events that led them to this place. At the end of it all, Brody was shaking his head, his expression one of disbelief.

"That's messed up."

"A little," Gene conceded. "And the reason why, as much as I'd like to pursue my vendetta against you, Reid and the others, I need to call a temporary truce."

"Why does it have to be temporary?"

Gene rolled his eyes. "Oh, not you too. Boris already fed me some bullshit line about forgiving me and welcoming me back into the goddamned fold. You and I both know that can't happen."

A speculative gleam entered Brody's gaze. "Why not? I'll be honest. You don't seem too angry to me, else we wouldn't be talking right now and my brains would be decorating the ground outside. I saw the gun in your ankle holster, yet you chose to wrestle with me instead of pulling it and finishing me."

"Maybe I wanted to squeeze the life out of you with my bare hands."

"Or maybe you don't really want to permanently hurt any of us but just don't know how to let go of the past. You know, I remember a time when a certain group of men had a theme song."

"A drunken jest," Gene said, a wry grin on his lips.

"But a boisterous one, one that we all meant."

"If you start singing Lean the Fuck on Me, I will kill you," Gene warned.

Slapping a hand over her mouth, Vicky suppressed a giggle and struggled to hold it in, especially when Brody grinned mischievously and opened his mouth as if he were about to belt it out.

"Brody!" Gene yelled his name. "Don't make me throttle you with my bare hands."

"Fine. I won't sing. It would be too cruel to your lady friend if I did. What's even crueler, though, is letting you think you gotta keep hiding to stay alive when you've got buds, who, after a little one-on-one stress relief, will want to lend you a hand."

"I don't need help. Like I said before, associating with me puts you in danger. The smart thing for you to do right now is pretend you never saw me and walk away."

It puzzled Vicky to hear that, and then again it didn't. Anyone could see dealing with his old friend tore at Gene, the longing and remembered fondness shining forth whether he meant it to or not. But also all too evident was Gene's implicit worry that he'd cause harm to those close to him.

Anything that scares Gene is something to not take lightly. What on earth could spook a fearless man like her hero?

"I'll admit, I'm not fond of danger, even if the adrenaline rush can't be beat. But I also can't just walk away. First off because my reason for being here was to find you. Can you imagine what would happen if Reid found out I'd let you go your merry way? He would skin me and use me as a carpet if I let you go."

"A mangy one."

"Insults won't send me packing, Ghost. Nor will dire premonitions. You need help. You need help finding the person behind the attacks on Vicky here and help staying alive if what you say about this big, bad enemy is true."

"Are you offering to aid us?"

"Yes. And not just me."

"You're not suggesting what I think you are?" asked Gene, his brow furrowing.

Once again a spectator, Vicky tried to fathom the undercurrents. But failed. She got the impression she was missing a whole layer of meaning, some vital fact that would enable her to understand exactly what transpired. Then again, given her previous analysis of men and their actions, she didn't know squat. Perhaps she just imagined tension that wasn't truly there.

"I think you and Vicky should come back with me to Kodiak Point."

"Are you out of your fucking mind?" Gene practically shouted.

Brody hooked his thumbs in the loops of his pants. "Nope. Last time I looked, I still had my wits. Boris, that big fucking moose, though, we're still unsure about. And as for you, apparently they need shaking loose."

"I'm perfectly sane, asshole, and intelligent enough to think it's a bad idea. I'm not going with you."

"Why not?" It wasn't Brody that asked but Vicky. She stepped closer to Gene and placed her hand on his arm, which tensed at her touch. "We could use the help."

His arctic gaze met hers, the ornery hero currently in charge. "You need the help. I need to stay the fuck away. If *he* comes after me, anybody in his way, anybody he thinks are my friends or allies will get hurt."

"Unless we stop him. I don't know who the fuck it is that's got you so wigged out, dude, but give us a little fucking credit. We're not some candy-assed recruits anymore. We've seen and done shit. We know how to defend ourselves and aren't afraid to use deadly force. Whoever it is gunning for you—"

"You, your mates, your family, your friends. The whole fucking town," Gene interrupted.

"Whoever it is," Brody firmly reiterated, "he obviously has no idea who he's messing with. Alone, we are weak, but together—"

"—we are clan," Gene finished with a sigh.

"More than clan. Family. And family doesn't let anyone get fucked, even stupid dickheads with a tree up their ass."

"I earned that tree."

At least Gene didn't deny it, Vicky thought with an inner giggle.

"Wah-fucking-wah. You can cry me a river later. We've all got issues. Now's not the time to piss and moan about them. So, we got a deal? Are you coming with me?"

A snort slipped out of Gene. "Deal? When did we negotiate?"

"Oh yeah. I guess I should lay out terms. We head back to Kodiak Point in the morning in my truck. Once there, we'll figure out who is attacking your lady."

"How?"

"I've got hacker friends," Brody said with a sly smile. "If he left an electronic trail, we'll find it. So once we solve Vicky's problem, then we'll sit down, like grown fucking men, and discuss, over gallons of beer, what the fuck happened overseas. You're not the only messed-up one. And I think it's about time we had ourselves an inter-fucking-vention."

"By getting a bunch of psychotic ex-soldiers in a room together where there will be alcohol and bad blood? That's just asking for a fight."

Brody nodded, "Yup. A big one."

"Just like the old days," Gene said with a smile.

"Exactly. Clear the air. Wipe out grievances."

Vicky could only blink as they calmly discussed a drunken riot with happy smiles.

"And then?" Gene asked.

"Then, old friend, we're going to lay a second trap, one for a bigger prize."

Listening to them, Vicky couldn't help but rejoice that Gene seemed to have found an unexpected ally, yet at the same time, as they spoke, she couldn't help but wonder what would happen to her. *Where will I be once whoever is behind the attacks is gone?*

Back home where I've got classes to attend, papers to write, and endless hours of programming on my DVR.

The answer depressed her.

Chapter Nineteen

Given some of the things Gene and Brody had to discuss were of a sensitive nature—ahem, inappropriate recollections in some cases of pranks they pulled while in the service—Gene ended up leaving Vicky in the room with the firm admonition of, "Don't open the door for anyone."

As an added precaution, when he and Brody hit the main floor of the small bar, they glared at the humans closest to the stairs until they wisely changed seats.

Placing himself in the worn chair with his back to the wall and a direct view of anyone who might try to approach the stairs for the second floor, Gene watched and brooded. While not a big town, the bar was a hot spot for inhabitants, a gathering place for the locals to hang out, drink and relax.

Brody, without a care, and way too much trust, leaned against the bar, his back turned, as he waited for their drinks.

I could slip out of here and be gone before he noticed.

Escape beckoned. A return to his solitude waited only a few feet away. But that would mean leaving Vicky behind. Alone. A magnet for trouble.

Brody wouldn't ditch her. He's got too much honor for that.

But would he protect her with his life? Would Brody get to the bottom of Vicky's troubles and take care of it or hand her over to human authorities and let them deal with it?

Drumming his fingers on the table, Gene sighed. He also didn't move his ass. When it came to Vicky, he lost all common sense. *I've become an idiot*, one who'd probably end up getting killed, but unless he was overseeing her safety himself, Gene didn't trust anyone else to handle it right. *And I don't know if I would forgive myself, or others, if she came to harm because I prefer stewing in solitary misery.*

Ignoring the interested stares of the few women populating the place, Brody returned holding two beers and slid into the mismatched wooden chair across from Gene.

Taking a sip, Gene watched his old friend through hooded eyes, waiting for him to speak.

Brody didn't hesitate. "I'm surprised you didn't bolt."

"I thought of it."

"But?"

Gene shrugged. "But decided I'd prefer to irritate you by sticking around."

"I feel so special. However, I have a feeling it has more to do with the lady upstairs than an urge to rekindle a friendship with me."

"I don't know what you're implying. There's nothing between us."

"If you say so. I gotta know, though, after hearing your story, how the hell does she not know your secret?"

"I wasn't kidding when I said she faints. A lot. Although she is getting better. When I first met her, she face planted if you so much as said 'boo'."

"Still… I mean, how many times is she going to meet a scarred polar bear followed by a naked you before she puts two and two together?"

"Denial is as powerful as a scientific mind." Gene hoped Vicky never found out he and the bear were the same. He didn't fear her spilling his secret. In that he trusted her. However, he would hate for the fear to re-enter her expression when she looked at him. To associate the big scary bear with the man.

But she loves bears.

There was a difference between loving an animal and knowing a man turned into an animal. Humanity often feared that which they could not understand. Those that feared too much and threatened to tell? Unfortunately, shifter justice showed them no quarter.

Vicky's response would only matter if she were to discern the truth.

As if the truth has stopped her so far. Tell her a crazed killer wanted him dead and she was more concerned he get help, and from the last place he expected, Kodiak Point.

"So what makes you think Reid will go along with the plan you laid forth upstairs? You might be his clan beta, but as alpha, the decision is ultimately up to him. How do I know you're not trying to march me voluntarily into a trap?"

"Give me a little credit. I wouldn't make such a big move if I didn't think he'd roll with it. Reid's cool with the plan."

"And you know this how?"

"Because I texted him while at the bar."

"Can't have been a long conversation," Gene replied dryly, "seeing as how the guy practically served you right away."

"Didn't need to say much. See for yourself." Brody extended his cell phone, and Gene perused the lit screen, which showed the conversation bubbles for Papa Bear—*don't snicker aloud*—and Big Bad Wolf. Brody employed interesting contact names.

Fnd g. Bk tmrw w/ hm. No kill. Cl mt.

Which for the rest of the world who couldn't follow Brody's severely curtailed texting stood for "Found Gene and will be back tomorrow with him and a human who doesn't know. Don't kill him. Call a clan meeting."

Reid's superbly worded alpha leader reply? K.

It brought home just how much trust some of the guys had in each other. For Reid to accept Brody's assessment, to place such value on it, reminded Gene of a time when he'd felt the same way.

How could I have changed so much as to want to hurt the ones I once loved like brothers?

Perhaps he should have gone to more than one session with the shrink after he'd returned to the real world after spending so much time in captivity. The shrink tried to tell him his anger wasn't with the guys but an expression of his frustration. Gene didn't like that reply and never went back. Could have partially had to do with the fact he'd held the little man by his ankles out of his window, shook him, growled, and told the guy to get some better answers before his next session. Despite their minor difference of opinion, he had decided to give the headshrink a second chance, except he was never allowed back on account of the restraining order.

He ditched therapy as a solution.

However, now he had to wonder if he should have stayed the course and maybe worked through some of the angry knots currently unraveling in his mind.

He wondered how much of his anger was merited and how much was a result of the mind fucking by the one who'd saved him? The sly bastard who'd whispered during more than one sibilant conversation that his friends had abandoned him. His friends didn't give a shit. His friends were never his friends.

Fucking brainwashed. And not really recognizing it until now.

Discovering you might be wrong? That needed another beer. And another. Which helped loosen the tongue, and while they skirted certain issues, he and Brody spent a pleasant few hours reminding themselves of the better times. The time when they tranquilized Boris' moose ass and then decorated his rack with Christmas bulbs and tinsel. Or the time they'd greased their rhino sergeant's baton so that when he went to rap it against something while yelling they were "lazy fucking princesses", it slipped his grip, spun in the air, and bonked him in the snout. So worth the hundred push-ups.

While a certain aura of tension and wariness remained, along with watchfulness every time the door to the bar opened, the fact he was actually sitting down and spending time with someone, and enjoying it, blew Gene away. A man used to his solitude, he'd forgotten the simple enjoyment of just shooting the shit with another person. Just like he was discovering the pleasure in having a female companion by his side.

A little drunk, not a lot because his big bear ass could quickly metabolize copious amounts of alcohol, he stated, "This is fucked up."

"What is?"

"Us. Here. Hanging." Not dragging the corpse of the other somewhere for disposal.

Leaning back on two of the chairs legs, which was really brave considering their ramshackle state, Brody replied, "No more fucked up than you shacking up with an oblivious human."

"We're not shacking up."

"But there is something between you," insisted Brody.

Yes there was, a tingling awareness, a definite chemistry, a stupid bond he couldn't seem to sever. But he'd not thought it that obvious, which bothered Gene. If Brody could see it, would his enemy spot it too? *And use it against me.*

Gene tried to deny it. "She's a hot little thing, but nothing can come of it. Not with the danger I have following me around. As soon as I can, I'm going to take off again."

"Ditching her might not lessen the danger."

"Keeping her is out of the question. We're too different."

"Maybe that's what you need," Brody replied before taking a sip of his beer. "Some relationships work best when there's lots in common, like Boris and Jan. Those two are the funniest gun freaks you ever met. I swear, between the pair, I don't know who owns more weapons.

"Jan. She inherited most of her dad's collection when Jean Francois began traveling."

Brody snorted. "Oh man. I am so totally going to use that against the moose when I see him.

His woman is the one who wears the guns in his relationship."

"It will drive him ballistic."

They both grinned at that thought.

Brody spun the brown bottle on the table, watching it wobble. "Then there's opposites, like Tammy and Reid. She was a human insurance adjuster and he the big bad bear in charge of our clan."

"You mean she was a human. She's now almost as big of a bear as him." Kind of his fault since, as part of his vendetta, Gene had changed her into a polar bear. Not something done often by his kind because of the level of danger involved. It was also very painful. His Pima would never survive the change from human to shifter. But then again, he didn't care if Vicky was human. He liked her just fine the way she was. Too much actually.

"The point is, different backgrounds and interests don't mean shit. When it comes to love—"

"Whoa!" Gene held up a hand. "Hold on a second there, Mr. Fucking-in-touch-with-his-feelings Freak. Who said anything about love?"

"Are you going to lie to me and say you don't feel anything for the girl? That the reason you're doing this is out of the kindness of your fucking heart?"

"Why not? I'm capable of being nice." At least for one person.

"Nice, yes, but stick around longer than needed and for a human?" The noise that came out of Brody could only be called scoffing. "The ghost I knew would emerge from the shadows only long enough to maybe kill a few things and avert danger. Then he'd ditch her ass and move on."

"Who says that's not what I'm planning?" He'd get Vicky to Kodiak Point, ensure the clan surrounded her with protection, and then he'd take off. A great plan.

"If you say so." Brody yawned. "I don't know about you, Ghost, but I think it's time we hit the hay. So sleeping accommodations. How about you take first watch, and I'll sleep with the girl in the room."

So fast did Gene traverse the table that his hand latched around Brody's neck before the chair he'd sat in finished thumping the floor. "Stay away from her," he growled.

Brody arched a brow. "Possessive much?"

Apparently more than he suspected. Or was it just the alcohol talking? Gene's control over his bear was a little tenuous at the moment it seemed. Its jealousy over the human it considered his forcing its way past his manly control. "You're not sleeping with her."

"I think that's patently clear. I take it I'm doing my sleeping and watching in the hall?" Brody inquired.

Gene could only grunt as he hefted himself off Brody and got to his feet. Without a word, he headed up the stairs, still slightly drunk, his mind definitely churning with a multitude of revelations and suddenly lustier than a bear in fucking spring.

Vicky was up there. In a room. In his bed. Not wearing several layers of clothes.

The sane part of him, which screamed he should head for a polar swim, understood that temptation awaited. The wilder side, the part of him controlled more by impulse and instinct, kept his feet moving. Had him staring down at her sweet features, evident by the soft glow of the sign lighting the outside.

He knew if he wakened her with a kiss, she'd return it. Knew if he decided to seduce her, here and now, she'd welcome it. Welcome him.

What does she see in me? Something obviously that he'd not spotted. She kept calling him hero, and as much as he—and yes Brody—might scoff, he enjoyed it. Pride warmed him knowing she felt as if she could count on him.

But would she sing the same tune if she truly saw him for what he was? *She knows I'm a killer.* A human killer. Could a delicate natured girl like her, though, handle the beast?

His cock twitched as her lips parted and she sighed in her sleep. *I didn't mean handle that kind of beast,* he thought with a smile.

Another smile. Because of her.

Stripping to just his long johns—the sexiest nightwear around—he slid onto the mattress alongside her, playing with fire, but he didn't care. Leaning on an arm, his head cradled in his palm, he stared at her features. Dark lashes, an upturned nose, luscious pink lips, mussed hair that feathered her cheek. He stroked the stray strands from her soft skin. She let out a sigh, and her lips parted.

Did she know he touched her?

He let his fingers glide lightly from her cheek to her jaw, tracing its line down the column of her neck. The blanket, tucked around her shoulders, impeded further progress, so he tugged it, pulling it down to see she wore those damnable polar bear jammies again. The one-piece pair with the zipper down the front.

Gripping the tag, he slowly tugged, the whirring sound loud in the stillness of the room, a warning that he should stop.

What are you doing?

She slept, and here he was taking advantage of her vulnerability. He stopped, and was about to zip her up, when she rolled to her side and murmured in her sleep. One word. Just one. A word that shredded rationality.

"Gene."

His name. *She's saying my name.* Despite her slumber, she knew it was him or dreamed of him. Something within him tilted. Or maybe the whole world did. All he knew was something huge changed in that moment, or perhaps it already had and he'd just noticed it.

I care for her.

Not just because she needed his help. Or because it was the right thing to do. He cared for her because she meant something to him.

The revelation stunned. His hand cupped her cheek, the thumb gently stroking the skin.

Lashes fluttered as her eyes opened to half-mast, soft and sleep-filled. Her mouth curved into a welcoming smile. "Gene."

Again, she said his name, this time cognizant. And demanding. Or so the arms she raised to snake around his neck indicated as she pulled him down to place a kiss upon his lips. A soft kiss, but one that aroused every one of his senses.

He took over the embrace, deepening it, demanding more. She eagerly gave in, her mouth granting him access so their tongues could twine and he could suck. He gathered her close to him with an arm around her back, pressing her against his chest, needing to feel her close to him.

But fabric dared get in the way of what he truly wanted. Skin-to skin contact.

There was no hesitation this time when he tugged her zipper. Vicky aided him in peeling the flannel garment just like her fumbling hands helped him strip out of his shirt and pants. Bare, he could finally do what he'd dreamt of since that first night when he'd held back. He could rub against her naked flesh. Rub and stroke and know he could enjoy it. He could touch it. He could…holy hell, he could finally taste her!

Once the idea hit his feverish mind, he couldn't shake it loose. Nor did he want to. It became imperative he discover the flavor of her cream. His lips left hers, despite her plaintive cry, a cry that turned into a moan as he dragged his lips down the column of her neck to the valley between her breasts.

Her breasts!

How could he have forgotten his fantasy about those? Delay his journey for some berries or continue?

Such a hard decision, decided for him by the musky aroma of her arousal. Taste. Now. He'd come back for his budding dessert later.

Downwards his mouth travelled, over the rounded swell of her belly, pausing to circle his tongue around her navel, which had her giggling his name.

"Gene!" She wiggled as he teased her one more time round the sensitive spot. He marked it for play later.

He continued his erotic trek, nuzzling the soft down covering her mound, the scent of her so strong now, so tempting. Her thighs parted for him with only the barest pressure from his hands, and he nestled between them, eyes closed in rapturous delight at the first lick.

Holy fuck, and he'd thought heaven was denied to him because of his past actions. Apparently not because he found it between her legs, he found it in her bliss-filled cries, discovered nirvana in the way her sex clenched around his fingers as his tongue stroked at her swollen nub.

Her hips bucked and lifted from the mattress, her pleasure turning her wanton and wild. So unlike his prim Pima, and oh so much more sexy for it.

Who knew his glasses-wearing, shy Latina hid a sex kitten inside? A kitten that tugged at his scalp and squeezed his head tight between the vise of her thighs.

The evidence of her enjoyment drove him wild. He lapped faster, his tongue stroking and his lips tugging while his fingers dipped in and out. The moment when she came? When she screamed his name? *MINE!* And her whole sex clenched then rippled around his fingers?

Almost as great as when he finally couldn't take it anymore and slammed his cock into her still undulating channel.

The moist flesh of her sex clamped down around his cock, and he threw back his head and hissed. "Oh, Vicky. My sexy, sexy Vicky."

She didn't reply, but she welcomed his thrusts, her arms once again twining around his neck to pull him down for a scorching kiss as he pumped into her, the milking of her pussy around his cock making him shudder as he struggled to hold on.

He wanted, needed her to come with him, so he held off on his own climax, instead stroking her warm, tight sheath with long strokes. Deep thrusts.

She clung to him, panting and matching his rhythm.

He lost the latch of her mouth but only because he had another destination in mind. The hard berries topping her breasts had poked his chest, reminding him of his earlier curiosity.

Dessert time.

It took a bit of arching and bending, but he managed to capture a tip with his mouth. He tugged the erect nipple, sucked it, and she let out a mangled moan. Her pussy spasmed around his cock. Damn did that feel good. So he did it again. And again. He swapped breasts, spreading around the sensual torture.

The tension in her body coiled. Her channel tightened. His thrusts sped up, and this time when she came, he came with her. He shot his seed deep inside. Marking her. Claiming her.

He roared his possession. He shouted it aloud, heedless of whom he woke. In that moment, he wanted the world to know she was his. *Mine.*

And beware any who tried to come between them.

However, what was he to do when the biggest barrier keeping them apart was him?

Chapter Twenty

Having already slept a few hours before Gene returned to make wonderful love to her, the last thing Vicky wanted to do after the most glorious orgasm ever—and she meant ever—was fall asleep.

So when Gene rolled on to his back and dragged her with him, draping her over his chest like a fleshy blanket, she took the moment to talk.

"I wasn't sure you'd come back," she admitted, the intimate darkness giving her the courage to voice the thing that plagued her most when he'd left the room.

"To be honest, I thought about going."

Not exactly the most encouraging revelation. "What made you change your mind?" she asked.

For a moment, she thought he wouldn't answer, and the silence stretched and stretched. He uttered a heavy sigh. "In the end, I couldn't just leave you. Not with everything going on. I had to make sure you were safe."

"And that's the only reason you stayed?" Yes, she fished for something a little cozier than his sense of duty. The disappointment when it wasn't forthcoming might have hit her harder if he hadn't been lightly stroking her back as he replied.

"Yes. No. I don't fucking know why. Must you ask? Can't we just leave it at I'm here?"

"For now," she finished. "But what about once we get to this place Kodiak Point and we solve the mystery? What then? You'll leave?" *Leave me* was what she wanted to say.

A part of her hoped for a vehement denial. A declaration that he would never leave her. Ever. But this was Gene.

"There are things you don't understand."

Not again! She was getting mightily tired of this oft-repeated refrain. "Then help me to understand. Tell me or explain." She leaned up until she could stare him straight in the eye, without fidgeting, fainting, or a single tremor. Clear-gazed and with determination. Possibly a first for her. As was the bravery she mustered to declare, "I know you feel something for me. I think I deserve a better explanation than *because* or *it's for your own safety*," she said mimicking a deep, grave voice. "Danger is around me everywhere, Gene. I could get killed crossing the street. Or from an aneurism. Heck, given how often I seem to run into them, even the wildlife or a polar bear could take my life with a swipe of its paws."

"Not if I'm around," he growled.

"But that's just it, according to you, you won't be around, and you won't even tell me the real reason why."

"I wish I could. There are things about me I can't explain. Things that would frighten you if you knew. Dangerous things."

Rolling her eyes probably wasn't mature, but it matched her mood. "Like what? What haven't I seen?" she asked with incredulity. "I mean, let's recap shall we the items I've discovered so far? I've seen you naked in the freezing cold. I've heard you cuss. Seen you fight. Kill. Heck, I even saw you pee while we were traveling. What else is left?"

"You wouldn't believe me if I told you. And you'd faint if I showed you."

She ogled him, sure she'd heard wrong. She'd seen him naked. Touched him. What could he possibly mean by show? "Show me what? What can you possibly have hidden that you think would chase me away?"

"It's big."

She wiggled. "Yes it is."

The O of shock on his face was totally worth her burning cheeks at her daring innuendo.

"Saucy woman." A grin curved his lips. "I see my bad influence is rubbing off."

"More like in."

He chuckled. "What am I going to do with you?"

"Do? How about trust me? Trust me to handle whatever it is you're still hiding. Trust me to accept it the way I've accepted everything else about you. I—" She swallowed as she hesitated, afraid of rejection, but even more afraid of not saying anything. For once in her life, if ever there was a time to speak up, it was now. Gene had proven he would torture himself rather than give in. But maybe if he heard how she felt… "I want us to stay together. I care about you, Gene."

"As in a couple?"

Did he have to sound so surprised? She nodded.

"You have seen how I live?" Again with more incredulity.

She nodded again.

"You do realize I am a killer."

"Yes. But you're not a bad man."

The sound he made could only be labeled as scoffing. "Only you would say or think that. The rest of the world sees me for what I am."

"I don't care what they think. The world thought my husband was a nice guy, but he was a jerk behind closed doors."

"Whereas I'm a jerk in public," he teased.

"More like gruffly assertive," she sassed back. "However, I like that about you. I like that you don't wear a mask. So whatever it is that has you thinking you need to run from what we have between us, running from me, can't be that bad. Tell me, Gene. Tell me what's really holding you back."

"Trust." He blurted the word out.

She frowned. "You don't trust me?"

"I do. But, if I let you in on my secret, I don't know if you still will."

He feared his secret would make her turn from him? Silly man. What could be worse than knowing he was a killer? "Give me some credit. I might be faint-hearted, but I'm not shallow."

"No, but you're human."

A comment that made no sense. Only human was what they all were. Flawed, human, and capable of acceptance despite differences.

He let out another of his heavy sighs. "Are you sure you're ready for this?"

Surely she could handle whatever big secret was left. *I don't care what it is if I get a chance to prove to him that we can be together.* Because more and more, the very idea of going their separate ways brought a crushing pain to her heart.

Somewhere along their journey, Vicky had fallen for this gruff bad boy. Violent, crass, caring, and oh so sexy, Gene was proving to be everything she wanted in a man and a companion. Yeah, he didn't always talk a lot, but then again, she wasn't a chatterbox. As for his love of this remote part of the country? Hopefully she could talk him into getting at least a house, with actual plumbing, but other than that, so long as she had her books and the Internet, she could see herself enjoying the quiet lifestyle, especially if it meant spending it with Gene.

If their enemies didn't get them first.

But that wasn't the *big secret*—and, yes, she mentally finger quoted. So what on earth could he consider awful enough that he didn't think she'd want to stay with him?

Is he dying of some incurable disease? Incapable of having children? Married already?

Hmm, all of those were enough to give her pause, but the real reason proved to be something far, far more unexpected.

Chapter Twenty-one

Do I show her? Brody seemed to think she could handle it. She had adapted well so far to everything else that had happened to her, but he was about to skew her whole perception of reality. *I'm about to let her know that the world she thought she knew and understood has monsters.*

Could she handle it? Or was the truth not about her, but him? *Maybe the person who can't handle it is me.* Because he feared she'd turn her back on him. That the sweet trust he so enjoyed in her eyes would change.

Then again, how was him ditching her and running away any better? In the one scenario, he was out of her life always wondering what could have been, and in the other, she would flee from him frightened. What about the third option? The one where she saw him for who he was and accepted it?

He could almost feel his sarge's spittle as he yelled, "*Stop your fucking belly aching, soldier, and man up.*" Gene took a deep breath and uttered his dark secret. "I am a polar bear."

There. He'd done it. Stated it aloud. No taking it back. The bare truth. Now for the deciding moment.

Vicky cocked her head and wrinkled her nose. "I don't get it."

"I. Am. A. Polar. Bear." Because surely stating it slowly would help her grasp the concept.

"What is that, like your Chinese animal or something? Because I've never heard of the zodiac having a bear."

How obtuse could she be? There was denial, and then there was his woman. Gene almost smacked himself in the forehead. "Holy fuck, Pima. Do you intentionally do this to drive me nuts?"

"I don't get it. I mean, you keep saying you're a bear, and, yes, I'll grant that you're grumpy and growly and stuff. But—"

Her voice trailed off, and her eyes grew wide as he showed her. Already naked, he didn't have to strip, and while their room wasn't the biggest, he had no problem shifting.

Skin rippled as fur sprouted. Lush white fur. Hands and fingers turned into paws with claws. His face elongated into a muzzle, and he grew in size and height until he sat, in all his polar awesomeness, before her.

To her credit she didn't faint. Nor did she scream. As a matter of fact, she didn't do a damned thing. Not blink or breathe or move.

Had she died of shock? No, because he could hear her racing heart.

Unable to speak, and wary of even the lowest growl lest he freak her out even further, he waited.

After what seemed like an eternity, she let loose a breath and uttered, with some amount of awe, "Holy fuck. You're a fucking polar bear."

The foul language coming from his naked Pima, as she sat crossed-legged on his mattress, would have made him laugh as a man, but as his bear, he could only snort and chuff.

If possible her brows crawled higher on her forehead. "You're a bear. *My* bear. It was you all along. You were the one always saving me."

The scar gave him away.

He was prepared for many things, more shock, maybe some fear, perhaps even a bit of awe—because his beast truly was magnificent. However, the flinging of her arms around his neck as she hugged him tight and buried her face in his fur? Yeah, he totally wasn't prepared for that.

"I can't believe you thought this would scare me off," she murmured in his fur. "You're so gorgeous. And strong. And a bear!" She said this as if it were the most wonderful thing ever. "I love polar bears. Oh my god. I have so many questions for you. Which I guess you can't answer right now, but I totally intend to ask when you're a man again. Or are you a man? Is there a name for you? Like werebear? And how did you get this way? Can you change whenever you want?"

As Vicky babbled, Gene mentally sighed. Now what? He'd expected his deep secret to send his Pima in to a fit. He just never expected it to unleash such a chatterbox. One who accepted him.

Holy shit. *She accepts me.* As he was. Scars, bear, foul-mouthed, and ornery. And she cared about him. She'd said so, and he knew she didn't say it lightly. He'd seen and heard the tremulous bravery as she admitted it. Knew the courage it took for her to say it aloud.

It made him want to shift back and sweep her into his arms and tell her the words back. Because, dammit, despite his determination to remain aloof, he'd fallen for this woman. Fallen hard.

When she'd asked him what would happen once the danger to her was gone, if he'd leave, he'd wanted to shout never. *Never will I leave your side.* Only years of habit held his tongue. A reminder of who he was curtailed his enjoyment of her declaration.

Yet, what if there was no danger to her, to him, to them? What if he decided to forgo his plans for vengeance and instead took the forgiveness and offer to come home that Brody and the others offered? Could he start over? Could he have a life with Vicky?

The door to his room slammed open, and Gene whirled with a snarl. He stayed his paw, though, before ripping Brody's face off. His friend's next words did little to diminish the sudden adrenaline rushing through his system.

"We've got company. Some already furry and those that haven't shifted are armed. Given they're skulking outside trying to cover all exits, I'd wager they are probably not up to any good."

A low rumble shook Gene's chest. *Nothing like a dose of reality to remind a man why he can't have a happily ever after.* It seemed his enemies had finally tracked him down.

But they'd never capture him alive.

"Are they after me or Gene?" Vicky asked.

"I'd say Gene given they're shifters, but as you're covered in his scent, you'll probably be a target too. I might suggest you get dressed and grab a gun."

"A gun?" She squeaked the word, her fear palpable, but when no thump followed, Gene silently congratulated her on reining in her fear.

"Yes, a gun. Oh and don't forget to lock the door."

As clothing rustled, Gene head-butted Brody toward the door. His friend took the hint and hit the hall, waiting for Gene's ass to clear the portal before closing it behind them. The click of the lock engaging showed his Pima was at least paying attention. Not that a locked door would do much. At most, it was a flimsy barrier of protection, but honestly, if the attackers made it past him to the room, she was fucked no matter what.

So I'll just have to make sure I kill them all. Threaten him? That was one thing, but threaten his Pima? That was an invitation to die.

Given the windows on the second floor were small and inaccessible, it made more sense for him and Brody to meet the attackers on the main floor where they'd have room to maneuver. Of course getting his big polar bear ass down the narrow stairs caused a bit of mirth on Brody's part.

He snickered as he followed behind Gene. "I see all that seal hunting and lazing about on the ice packs has made someone's ass a little fat."

Growl.

"Need me to give you a shove so you can get down the stairs."

Snarl.

"Hope all that blubber doesn't impede your ability to fight."

Rumble.

"Mad yet?"

Yeah.

"Just in case you're not quite in berserker, polar-bear-rage mode, I think I should add I saw your woman naked. And man, does she ever have a nice set of tits. If you don't make it out alive, maybe I should make a play for her."

With a roar to shake the rafters, Gene didn't wait for the fight to come to him, not with the rabid ire thrumming through his veins. He took his ballistic need to kill something outside, charging through the front door, which Brody wisely flung open a moment before Gene turned it into kindling.

He took a pair of men armed with shotguns by surprise, tearing through them, and trampling before they could shout, "Holy shit!"

But once that initial element of surprise wore off, the fight was on.

When it came to battle, shifters were of two mindsets. One group, the naturalists he mockingly called them, preferred to fight in their animal form. They eschewed weapons and rules, preferring to engage in a blood-thirsty, savage duel to the death. Gene excelled at this type of fight.

Then there were the modernists, who could shift but preferred the calm precision and gore-spattering method of combat that allowed the use of guns, crossbows, or knives. A well-aimed shot, or perfect slice, could quickly incapacitate the enemy, leaving a fighter with more energy to survive numerous attacking waves.

Gene was real good at that too. He'd say just ask his enemies, but, well, there weren't really any left alive to crow about his prowess. And he'd long since stopped keeping body count.

And then there was a third state. The berserker rage. It was discovered that when Gene got really, really, really fucking mad, he could mix and match his skills via a half shift.

For example, while he began his mad dash outside as a bear and mauled the first two attackers, before the bodies had hit the ground, he morphed parts of himself, enough that he could stand upright and move like a man, his paws turned into hands, albeit still with hooked claws. The best of two worlds. Tear his enemy apart with his feral aspects or snag a gun from cold fingers and fire on the coward who thought to park himself across the street and take potshots.

Everything was a rush of sound, motion, screams, gunfire, darkness. In other words, utter chaos. The bartender, who owned the place and lived over the business, emerged in unlaced boots, a flapping flannel shirt, and red long johns wielding his gun.

Lucky for Gene, he wasn't hunting polar bear.

"Fucking varmints. Attack my fucking saloon, will you?" the old soldier yelled as he took aim at a wolf—not Brody—that tried to slink through the front door.

Speaking of Brody, he'd retained his man shape and was double-fisted, knife in one hand, pistol in the other. He ducked and swerved as he made his way around the side of the building, the distant screams letting Gene know he'd found more of the enemy to play with.

He let Brody have them. There was more than enough to go around.

It seemed *he* had finally tired of Gene's defection and had waited for him to surface. Just as Gene feared. Had he been alone, he would have ditched the town and his supplies, leading the bastards away from the settled area and the civilians getting caught in the crossfire. But Brody was here, and the idiot would never run from battle.

And then there was Vicky.

Poor defenseless Vicky, who probably huddled in his room, terrified. *I need to protect her.* Because he didn't doubt for an instant that *he* knew about her, and if *he* got his hands on her, she'd end up hurt.

Not while I live.

The very thought of her suffering any kind of injury fueled his rage. It helped him ignore the sting of a bullet that seared across his upper arm. It allowed him to block the pain as a wolf latched its teeth around his calf until he aimed a gun at its head and blew it off.

Everything was going great. Fuck, despite the odds, he, Brody, and the crazy soldier-turned-barkeep were winning. Bodies both human and not littered the area. Gene actually managed to pause and breathe for a minute or two when he heard it.

The scariest sound he'd ever heard in his life.

"Put me down, you brute."

Pima!

Chapter Twenty-two

Every smart geek knew, from watching movies and reading books, that if a hero said to stay hidden, then you should stay hidden. Nothing good came of venturing forth bravely, glasses firmly in place, some kind of blunt object in hand.

Knowing this, Vicky planned to stay in the room. She didn't harbor any illusions about her usefulness in a fight. Despite her burgeoning bravery, she'd prove nothing but a hindrance. With her luck, she would probably faint at the most inopportune moment.

Before she hid, though, she did prepare. She dressed in her warmest clothes, threw on her boots as well, grabbed a gun—which terrified her and she held gingerly lest she shoot her own foot off—and hunkered down in a corner.

Waiting, though, proved harder than expected, especially because she could hear the chaos happening just outside.

It frightened her; she couldn't stop that. Yet, in spite of her fear, she remained awake, even if she cringed at the screams and the crack of gunfire. While Vicky felt a little faint, her face didn't meet any hard surfaces, although her limbs did shake. Her bladder didn't betray her—yay, no need for an adult diaper yet—even as she heard the tread of heavy steps outside the door and the ominous rattle of the knob.

However, when something banged against that flimsy portal and it popped open to hit the wall with a crash, she did utter a small, frightened, "Eep!" She could have slapped herself for emitting the sound because it immediately drew attention from her unsavory visitor.

As the unshaven thug with cold eyes, a cruel smile, and the rifle in hand entered the room, she couldn't help but remain in a frozen huddle in her corner. The geek in her attempted to use a Jedi mind trick on him. *You see nothing. Go away.*

It didn't work.

A sneer twisted his lips, and his derision was clear when he spoke. "Well. Well. What have we here? The bear's whore. Won't the master be pleased?"

Someone give the man a dictionary. I'm not a whore by any sense of the definition. But she didn't say this aloud. Fear froze her tongue, and she could only hyperventilate as he came farther into the room, advancing on her.

Where was a bear, or Gene, or both when she needed them? If ever she required a hero, it was now. Like right now.

Any instant now.

Surely he'd come to her rescue. He always had before.

However, no towering Gene with a scowl appeared to remove the menace. No looming bear with a vicious snarl arrived in the nick of time. It was just her, and the thug who grinned victoriously.

Oh my god.

So this was what death looked like when it came for a girl. Unshaven, smelly, and in need of a dental plan.

I don't want to die like this. Not like a coward huddled in a tiny ball.

Suddenly she remembered her weapon. She swung the gun upward and aimed it at his chest. In a tremulous voice, Vicky said, "Go away." *Yeah, way to tell him.*

Not surprisingly, he laughed mockingly. "Or what? You and I both know you're too chickenshit to shoot. Why, you can barely hold that gun."

Given the shake of her hands and the wobble of the barrel, Vicky couldn't deny his words. *I am terrified, and, yes, I'm barely able to keep the stupid, heavy thing pointed.* But was she going to allow terror make her a victim?

No? was the feeble reply from her hiding inner heroine.

Not exactly encouraging. It seemed she lacked the gumption to believe in herself.

Faintness threatened as she panted, the tremors making her teeth chatter.

She drew in a breath. *No.*

A little better. Firmer. She could do this. *I can do this. I won't be a victim anymore.*

NO!

Her eyes closed and…

She fired, and almost got a black eye for her effort as the recoil almost smacked the gun in her face. As it was, her ears rang, her arms smarted, and she was still just as terrified, especially since a peek showed him still standing. She'd only nicked him in the arm, which he stared at with disbelief.

"You bitch! I'm going to fucking kill you for that," he growled.

She could almost hear Gene say, *"Not if I kill you first."* Do or die time. She chose do.

Eyes closed, she aimed in his general direction and fired again. And again and again…

When only clicks sounded in the room instead of the thundering boom, she peeked with one eye.

Nausea gripped her as she saw the result of her actions.

Him or me, she reminded herself. Better him.

But she couldn't stay here with the evidence of what she was capable of doing when she found her courage and her life was placed in jeopardy. The room had lost its safe-haven status, and she refused to sit here waiting for an outcome with a corpse—that according to horror movies would probably begin to twitch and come to life as an undead creature. Nice to see her vivid imagination was functioning at an elevated level.

Rising to her feet, she averted her gaze before stepping gingerly over the body. When it didn't grab her ankle as she crossed, she just about sighed in relief.

Keeping a wary eye on it—for any sign of freaky movement—she snagged a second gun she'd seen stashed in the side pocket of Gene's bag. New weapon in hand—safety switched off because, as Gene, in one of his rare talkative moments, had taught her, there was no point in having a gun to defend yourself if you couldn't use it. Speed could spell life or death. The thinking and time it took to fumble a safety latch off could make all the difference in a fight.

Funny the things you could remember when circumstances called for extreme survival.

As the dead body behaved and showed no signs of turning zombie, she tiptoed to the splintered doorframe. Taking a deep breath, she peered around the jamb, ready to jump and probably scream like a girl. Given her taut nerves, it wouldn't take much to send her in to a fit. Or wet her pants.

No need to panic. An empty hall gaped.

Whew. Breathe out. Still on her toes, dumb considering she wore big, less-than-dainty boots, she inched her way to the top of the stairs. She held tight to the gun with two hands, readying herself, and then peeked down.

Clear.

Look at me, sneaking around like a pro. Ha. She doubted pros clenched their Kegel muscles tight lest they pee themselves.

Step by step, gun held out like she'd seen in the movies, her ears ringing from the shots she'd already fired, she made her way down the stairs to the main level. Still not a soul around. Thank god.

Outside, she could hear the sounds of battle. Snarls from an animal, possibly Gene. The yells of human voices, the ringing retorts of gunfire. No way was she going out there. Self-preservation kicked in and told her to hide. But where? Not under a table. Behind the bar? In the washroom?

Before she could decide, company arrived.

"What do we have here?" exclaimed an unfamiliar voice from behind her. "Smells like bear to me."

What is it with these guys and their claiming I stink?

Before she could whirl and repeat her daring shooting, someone knocked the gun from her hand

and grabbed her. So much for defending herself. Her assailant easily overcame her flailing and flung her over a shoulder.

"Put me down, you brute," she yelled, which, not surprisingly, had no effect on the thug and yet didn't go entirely unnoticed.

The most vicious roar ever split the air.

Gene.

He heard her and came to the rescue, or so she assumed from her less-than-stellar position.

The guy holding her upside down over his shoulder tensed as he said, "Come any closer, bear, and the girl gets it."

By gets it, she assumed he meant shot by the round muzzle of the gun pressing against her ribs. *What are the chances he'll miss?* Not likely.

With all the blood rushing to her head, terror making her heart race fast enough to explode, and now this newest threat…Vicky finally gave up the battle to be courageous and let darkness claim her.

Chapter Twenty-three

Who dares touch what is mine!

At the sight of his Pima in the grips of the enemy, Gene morphed back to his man shape. His burning rage could have helped him to keep his deadly half-shifted form, but he hoped to appear less threatening to the asshole who dared lay hands on his woman.

Gene tried reasoning first. "Put the girl down, and I'll let you have a head start." A head start so he could chase his ass down and shove the head he planned to rip off up it.

"Head start? Cocky bastard, aren't you? Looks to me like I'm the one in the position to give orders. Tell you what, how about you drop the knife in your hand and I'll call in one of my buddies to handcuff you and then, maybe, I'll put the girl down. Oh, and let you watch as I have some fun with her."

Apparently someone didn't get the memo on not pissing Gene off. "You really don't want to do that," Gene calmly stated, even if cold fear iced his veins. It seemed there were still some things capable of scaring him, and a threat to Vicky was one of them. Given he hated weakness of any sort, he'd have to deal with it. And nothing banished fear better than death.

"I'd say that if you want the woman to live, you're not in a position to make demands."

The idiot before him might not know it, but he was wasting his last breaths on pompous statements instead of more useful words such as, *Please don't kill me*. "It wasn't a demand. It was an offer. Last chance, put the girl down."

"Fuck—"

The idiot with a death wish never got to finish the sentence as Gene moved too fast. Up came his arm. With absolute precision, the knife he held went flying. And hit.

Bull's-eye. Nothing killed faster than a blade through the eye socket. No healing from that wound.

I warned him. No one touches my Pima.

Before the body began to wobble, Gene darted forward and snagged Vicky's limp body.

His Pima had fainted. Not that he could blame her. Fighting in this scenario would have probably resulted in more harm than good.

As he cradled her in his arms, checking her for signs of injury, especially once he scented the blood on her clothes, blood that thankfully didn't belong to her, Brody arrived.

"Shit, where did this fucker come from?"

"Doesn't really matter. He's dead now, and the dead don't get up and walk away." *Not yet at any rate.* But he wouldn't put it past *him* to look for a way. Hell, his old master had figured out a way to get feral wolves and other wild beasts to follow his command. Who was to say zombies weren't next?

"Fuck me, you weren't kidding when you claimed the dude had a hard-on when it came to snuffing you. Which reminds me, what the hell is his name?"

Gene shrugged. "No idea."

"What do you mean no idea? How could you not know that, seeing as how you worked for him and all?"

"I wasn't kidding about *his* power. No one remembers *his* name. Or his face. Nothing other than the fact that *he* is one seriously evil dude." Gene had pondered this oddity about the one everyone called master. Considering himself pretty strong-minded, Gene couldn't fathom how, other than by impossible magic, a man—or not—could just make people forget any specifics about him as well as command wild creatures to do his bidding.

Mind control? Surely such a thing did not exist? He didn't mention his theories aloud.

"Sounds like some form of brainwashing. The doc might have some ideas about that."

Brody still spoke as if Gene would accompany him to Kodiak Point. After this attack… Gene veered the conversation. "How many came after us?"

"Fourteen by my count, along with some wild wolves, a few wild caribou, and some jackrabbits," snapped the barkeep, who entered the room with a limp.

Brody snickered. "Evil bunnies attack. Did they smack you in the shins with their big, floppy ears?"

The barkeep glared. "Does this look like the face of someone amused? When I agreed to rent you that room, I told you I didn't want any trouble."

Gene growled. "Watch your tone, old man. I've had a rough night."

"I'll speak any goddamn way I like. This is my bloody place, and because of you, it's got fucking gunshot holes in the walls and dead bodies all over. Not to mention, a rabid rabbit bit my leg. A wolf, that's respectable. A caribou gore, a fine battle wound, but getting chewed on by a bloody bunny, I won't have it. I want you out!"

"Not my fault you can't handle little woodland creatures." As Gene stood toe-to-toe with the barkeep, body bristling, Brody stepped between them.

"We're sorry for the trouble. My friend here didn't mean for this to happen. And we'll pay you for damages. Send the bill to me."

The barkeep only slightly relaxed his scowl. "Fucking right someone is going to pay. But it should be him." His pointed look didn't leave any doubt who the him was. Gene restrained an urge to punch him. "You're a good man, Brody. I don't know why you're sticking up for the likes of this fellow. Anyone can see he's got trouble written all over him."

Must. Not. Hit. Asshole. Gene was trying, really damned hard, to behave for Brody's and Vicky's sakes, but his patience rapidly melted.

"Watch your mouth when you talk about my friend," Brody stated in a low, menacing voice. "I'm not the only one who owes this man a debt. As a veteran for our country, he deserves some respect."

Gene almost choked. *Did he just jump to my damned rescue?*

Brody wasn't done. "We'll be leaving now. And if you know what's good for you, you won't breathe a word of our presence. If anyone asks, these bastards came out of nowhere and started fighting. They seemed drunk and the animals loopy. Maybe they came across a pocket of gas, something that drugged them and made them all a bit crazy."

"Who the hell is going to believe that?"

"Everyone because that's the story. We both know the only law enforcement in this town is one of us." Us meaning a shifter. "They'll file a report blaming a belch from Mother Nature. And that will be that. Because, if I hear otherwise, I'll make an example of you." Brody cracked his knuckles.

Having threatened—and done—worse, Gene wasn't impressed.

The barkeep was. "I'll keep my mouth shut."

"A wise plan," Gene replied dryly.

"Shut it, bear. I'm only agreeing because I don't want to start no trouble with Reid's clan. But you aren't welcome back."

"I wasn't intending on returning." Compromised hiding spots did him no good.

As Brody and Gene headed upstairs, Vicky still limp in his arms, the stench of death reached him. He couldn't help but pause in shock as he saw the bullet-riddled body in the room.

Vicky had to kill a man.

In self-defense, but still, if not for him, she would have never had to suffer the trauma of taking someone else's life.

Because of him, she would bear an emotional scar.

Worse, she ended up lucky. Gene knew things could have been much worse. *What if they'd managed to escape with her? What fate would she have suffered then?* His mind could visualize too many scenarios. None of them pleasant. All of them his fault.

I think my course is clear. But he didn't tell Brody. Not yet. First, Gene dressed, then he gathered his things and Vicky's before following Brody back down.

Outside police lights flashed, and it didn't take a genius to realize leaving through the front door wasn't an option. So they slunk out the back, the crisp night air not enough to revive his Pima. But, given how long her fainting spells lasted before, he gauged it wouldn't be long now.

And he wanted to be long gone before she turned her trusting gaze on him and made him falter in his resolution.

Damned woman makes me weak.

Brody's truck wasn't parked far away, and it took only a moment after he stashed her inside the cab before his old army buddy realized Gene didn't plan on leaving with him.

"You're not coming to Kodiak Point with me, are you?" Brody stated.

"No. The clan is under enough scrutiny and pressure as it is. If I return, it will just add to it."

"Whether you're with us or not, the dick you used to work for is going to cause shit. You know it, and I know it. So why would you choose to go it alone when we could face him together."

"I don't do together."

"Not even for Vicky?"

Gene's hands fumbled the straps to his backpack. "Especially because of Vicky. You saw what almost happened back there. She almost died."

"Almost. But didn't because you had me to back you up. Now imagine a whole town."

"Why are you doing this?"

"Doing what?"

"Arguing so hard for me to return. When you first bumped into me, you were determined to take me out."

"I thought we hashed the reasons out last night."

"Yeah and I still don't get it." Still couldn't understand how Brody and the others managed to forgive him. First Reid going easy on him even though Gene had come closest to killing him. Then Boris, letting him go and offering him absolution, and now Brody. Why could none of these assholes act like jerks? How was a man supposed to remember why he'd ever thought vengeance was the solution when they kept being so goddamned nice?

Like a cult, they kept trying to entice him back into their fold. *Come to Kodiak Point. We serve beer and forgiveness.* As well as an offer to help him strike back at the enemy who hunted him. "I'm better off alone."

"Friends don't let friends fight alone."

Friends? When was the last time he'd heard anyone use that term around him? It cracked the wall he'd built around himself just a little farther. It was what he blamed for what he said next. Words Gene had not said in a long time but now seemed to mete out a little too often for comfort. "Thank you."

Ack. Another person he owed. If this kept up, he'd end up with enough people for a goddamned Tupperware party or Saturday night guy's poker. Playing with bullets because none of them could be bothered to buy chips.

"You want to help me, make sure Vicky's safe. Find the asshole who hired those killers and, once he's taken care of, send her home. Where she belongs."

"Are you seriously just going to leave without saying goodbye?"

"Bye."

"Not to me, you fucking moron, to her. You know she'll be crushed if she wakes and you're not there."

Gene's resolve wavered. He channeled his sarge—*indecision is for the weak*—and bitch slapped it back into place.

"Tell her I said this was for the best."

Best for who though? he wondered as he walked away. Because it sure as hell hurt a heck of lot more than it should have.

Chapter Twenty-four

Days later…

No fucking way. Reading the newspaper headline didn't make the news any better.

Woman thought dead in rare polar bear attack on arctic expedition is found alive and well. Rescuers are baffled how she survived the extreme conditions and emerged in such good health. Despite the coma she's in, the doctor and residents of the area are claiming it's a miracle. While unable to travel home yet, Vicky Sanchez is being cared for by the doctor of Kodiak Point, a remote town in Alaska…

Un-fucking-believable.

The bitch survived yet another attack. Would nothing kill her nerdy fat ass? Millions sat in bank accounts, waiting to get inherited if only she'd croak.

But it seemed hired killers just weren't all they were cracked up to be.

How many times will she escape certain death?

Or was this a case where it was best to handle things in person? How hard could it be to kill a woman in a coma?

It would certainly save a buttload of money. The more the idea percolated, the more it appealed.

Time to crack out a parka, long johns, and boots. He was going to Alaska because, apparently, *if you want something done right, do it yourself.*

Chapter Twenty-five

A few weeks after the attack…

A coma would probably have proven less boring than this. Vicky couldn't help but sigh as she took a turn watching the security monitor.

"How much longer do you think we need to maintain this charade before your husband admits this plan to lure out my killer won't work?"

"Knowing Reid and his stubborn bear ass? I'd say when the polar caps melt," said Tammy, the new friend she'd made since her arrival in Kodiak Point. A short and curvy gal, like herself, the feisty wife of the clan leader had taken an instant interest in Vicky when she arrived woebegone and frightened.

"I can't stand all this waiting around, doing nothing," Vicky grumbled. While usually patient, she'd found herself a little less so since her recent adventures. Forget feigning happiness at twiddling her thumbs, she chafed at the boredom of maintaining watch.

"Yeah, inaction sucks. On the bright side, though, no attack might mean that whoever was trying to kill you gave up."

"Great." Vicky showed a definite lack of enthusiasm. Probably because so long as she stayed in Alaska, there was a chance, however slim, that Gene might return. Very slim she had to admit. Surely if Gene wanted to return, he would have by now.

The smart move, the one that her newly constructed pride suggested, would have involved her saying thank you to Reid and Brody for their offer of help and leaving for home. She didn't do it. Not out of fear of what might await her at home though, but more because she hadn't given up hope. Scratch that. She hadn't given up on Gene.

When she'd woken, drooling on the window of Brody's vehicle a few weeks ago, it took her a while to grasp that Gene had abandoned her. Given the night they'd spent, the things they'd said, and shared, she'd really not expected him to leave. And not just leave but to go without even saying goodbye.

During that long ride to Kodiak Point, in Brody's diesel-powered truck, she'd spent a lot of time peeking out the window at the side view mirror. Despite the improbability, she watched for a polar bear to come lumbering after them. Or for a familiar bulky figure on a snowmobile to race to catch them.

But as the miles went by, and the hours ticked on, that fantasy shattered.

Gene wasn't coming back. *I lost my cuddly polar bear.*

Without his gruff presence, she felt so alone. More alone than when her husband died. More alone than she'd ever felt in her life. Which made no sense. Yet, she couldn't help the feeling. Even with Tammy by her side and everyone in Kodiak Point so welcoming, Vicky missed her ornery bear.

Sigh.

"I'd offer you a penny for your thoughts, but I'd say they're pretty blatant. I still can't believe how hard you fell for Gene." Tammy couldn't help a moue of distaste, but Vicky couldn't blame her.

From what they'd told her, Gene had not only kidnapped Tammy to draw Reid into a trap, he'd changed her. As in, Tammy had moved from the human gene pool to the shapeshifter one.

The knowledge initially blew Vicky away. One, because the idea that someone could become an animal still seemed pretty crazy, and this in spite of the fact she'd seen it with her own eyes. And two, because she couldn't picture the Gene she knew causing that kind of pain to anyone.

Sure, he claimed he possessed a bad side—she'd certainly seen it in action—but the Gene Vicky knew would never do anything to hurt a woman.

Or at least he wouldn't hurt me. Physically, she amended. Emotionally, though, he'd torn her heart to shreds. Not that she let it show. Much. The only reason she didn't cry was because of years of practice. Her father and Rick had taught her that tears brought more punishment. So she held the pain inside but couldn't help her lackluster interest in what went on around her.

It helped she had distraction. When she'd arrived in Kodiak Point, she'd found herself welcomed, warned, and waiting all within hours.

Welcomed by Reid, the alpha of the clan—which was what they called a community of shapeshifters who chose to live together. Once she got past her urge to faint—the man had a certain intimidation factor—she spent a good hour or more telling him everything that had happened to her.

Right after that came the big warning by Reid, and some scary dude called Boris, who made it clear if she leaked any of the things she'd learned about shifters she'd end up feeding the wildlife. Or end up in Jan's stew pot. Apparently, Boris' wife had a really old recipe passed down from her mother for Spanish Conquistador soup. Vicky didn't think it prudent to mention she was of Latina descent. With her juicy thighs and padded ribs, she didn't want to tempt them in case they had an even tastier recipe.

Then came the waiting. Waiting for something to happen as they dangled her as bait in the hopes of drawing out whoever was determined to kill her.

But she didn't wait alone. Tammy joined her. Even better though, Tammy was a polar bear and had, to Vicky's delight, posed for her and given her more than enough images and insight to write a half dozen papers—albeit minus the whole I-turn-furry parts.

If Vicky sounded blasé about her acceptance of shifters, it was because, despite their animal side, she quickly realized they were still people, just specially endowed ones.

Given what she knew of shifters now, it seemed all too obvious. Observing the townsfolk of Kodiak Point, who could ignore that there was something special about them? The way they moved, the look in their eyes…Wildness lurked in their gaze, and a certain fluid grace marked their movements. Overall, they possessed an air of confidence, of restrained wildness, and, at times, barely-in-check violence, which never failed to make Vicky shiver. *I'm surrounded by predators.*

Predators who'd pledged to capture the person behind the attempts on her life.

If that person was even still trying.

Back in the real world, albeit a chillier one in a more rustic town, Vicky had to wonder at all the things she'd experienced. Guys trying to drug her. A bear saving her. Gunshots. Gene turning into an animal.

Perhaps this was all some massive hallucination. Maybe she'd never made if off that ice shelf in the first place and lay there still, frozen and almost dead, her mind vividly—

"Ouch!" Vicky exclaimed as Tammy pinched her, shattering that illusion.

"Toughen up. Or as Boris would say, suck it up, buttercup. You'll need thicker skin than that if you're going to survive as a shifter's mate."

"A what?"

"Mate. You know as in significant other. The jam to Gene's peanut butter. The yin to his yang."

"Gene's not coming back."

"Don't count on it. Apparently, these guys are really big on fate and stuff, especially when it comes to hooking up. If you and Gene forged a connection like I think you have, then he'll be back. He won't be able to help himself."

Vicky wanted to believe her. Yet, hadn't her past taught her to expect only disappointment? She should have known better than to expect love, or even affection. Hadn't she learned her lesson when it came to men? If her own father and husband couldn't abide her, then why expect that a man like Gene would? In retrospect, it became clear Gene had helped her out of a sense of duty and slept with her because she was handy. *And because I threw myself at him.*

"It's best this way. He's right. We're too different. It would have never worked."

"What did I tell you about negative talk?"

"That you'd take me outside and give me a snowjob." Which, as Vicky discovered, involved having her face rubbed with snow until she squealed uncle.

Tammy grinned. "That's right. So chin up and think happy thoughts. He's coming back. I'll even wager on it. And speaking of coming back, I am starved. I'm going to hit the diner down the road for a bite. You want something?"

Her belly rumbled. "Sure. I could use something greasy."

"I knew I liked you for a reason," Tammy replied with a laugh. "Same toppings as usual?"

"Please."

"You got it. One greasy burger and fry coming right up. Remember to lock the door behind me."

The door being the one to an office at the other end of the medical facility, far from the room where Vicky supposedly lay in a coma. Bait for her killer.

As for who lay in the actual bed? A decoy wearing a wig with tubes taped to the face, the blankets drawn high and lights dimmed low so that a quick glance wouldn't give the ruse away.

The hope was by portraying her in the news as incapacitated they would draw either a new set of killers for questioning or the culprit himself, the identity of whom she still struggled with.

Discreet inquiries by Reid and Brody, even Tammy, who had connections in the insurance world, returned as dead ends. They couldn't discover who would benefit from Vicky's death. So their solution was to lay a trap.

Given the elaborate situation was about her, Vicky volunteered to help with the surveillance. Despite the gruff "No" Reid barked, Vicky stood her ground—without fainting, yay—and insisted on taking her turn watching the monitors.

Why not use a guard in the room? Because they didn't want to scare any attempts away. In order for their plan to work, they needed to make it seem as if she truly slept in that room. A guard would have roused suspicion.

Given the relative smallness of the medical facility, positioning men around it wasn't feasible, not without giving the ruse away, so they resorted on strategically placed cameras. At the first hint of something wonky, Vicky, or whoever was on watch, was supposed to call Boris, who headed the team of guys who would then swoop in and apprehend the attackers.

Gene would have killed them.

Because he was sweet and protective that way.

How she missed him, especially since he would have so enjoyed kicking some butt. With him around, she would have felt safe, protected, because, oh my god, wouldn't it figure the moment Tammy left, skulking forms appeared on one of her monitors?

She wouldn't have pegged them as bad dudes though, if not for the fact they'd managed to avoid getting caught on camera until they landed right outside her hospital room door. Well, not hers technically since she'd never slept in it, but they didn't know that. They hadn't come to say hello, not with the rope one held, the gun for another, and the malicious leer on the third as he opened the door.

What happened to the nurse on duty? Vicky flipped to another screen and fiddled with the various channels until she found the nursing station. She caught sight of white-sneaker-clad feet only for a second before a fourth fellow tucked them behind the counter.

Uh oh.

She scrambled for the phone and hit the number one on speed dial.

"Yeah," answered Boris, the word more like a grunt.

"Bad guys," she squeaked. "Here. Now." For those who might have mocked her oratory skills during this time of panic, she said bugger off. At least she was conscious.

"On my way."

Click.

Vicky double-checked the lock on the door. Engaged. It didn't make her feel any better. She paced the room while watching the screen. The lurking figures entered the room with the fake her and surrounded the bed.

Before they could act, Brody, whose turn it was to play possum, flung back the sheets and attacked.

His fist shot out and caught one in the midsection, doubling the guy with the rope in two. Rolling off the bed, Brody narrowly missed the swooping knife that embedded itself in the mattress.

Watching avidly, she couldn't help a scream of surprise when the knock came at the door. But Vicky didn't answer. She and Tammy had a system, which Boris insisted on. She waited for the code. A single rap, followed by three quick ones.

Tap. Tap. Tap.

She let out the breath she held and fumbled the lock until she could swing the door open.

Then she stood staring, jaw open, eyes wide, and a sick feeling forming a ball in her tummy.

"You."

"Yes. Me. Surprise, I'm not dead. But you soon will be," said Rick, her not-so-dead husband just before his fist connected with her jaw.

Chapter Twenty-six

Stay away. That was Gene's plan. Stay away from Kodiak Point. Stay away from Brody, Reid, and the rest. But most of all stay away from the one woman who'd upset his entire life. Who screwed with his emotions. The one person who dared to make him feel more than anger.

A woman who made him want to love.

He spent hours convincing himself she was better off without him and that she'd get over him—even if he doubted he'd ever forget her. He compiled a list of arguments as to why he should run far away and never return. It was a great list too.

Number one. Women expected romantic gestures. *My idea of romance is giving her oral.* Which she'd enjoy, but certainly wasn't the flowers and poems she'd probably expect.

Number two. Women wanted to live in houses, not shacks or in a tent on the run. *Although Pima didn't seem to mind much, and it wouldn't kill me to maybe get a more permanent place with plumbing.*

Number three. Gene hated sharing; his bed, his food, his guns. *Then again, cuddling at night was kind of nice, and watching her eat is arousing. As for letting her touch my guns...* Drool. Nothing hotter than a woman with a weapon.

Number four. He probably wouldn't live long with the enemies he'd made. *I could always kill them to keep her safe.* Lots of fun times there.

Number five. He'd probably end up with more enemies as he killed people in a jealous fit. *Mine. Mine. Mine. Don't look. Don't touch.* Possessiveness was no longer exclusive to items it seemed.

Such a great list of reasons to stay far away— with annoying rebuttals. Meanwhile, his other list extolling why he should go after Vicky had just one really compelling argument; *because I need her.*

Need but wouldn't let himself have, especially since the attack at the bar led him to believe associating with him put her at risk. Knowing this, Gene did his best to draw *his* attention elsewhere by placing himself in plain sight in various towns across Alaska.

It worked too. Attacks occurred, ambushes, assassination attempts. However, the quality of *his* army left much to be desired. It took way too little effort to kill those who tried to take him down.

But each minion he killed meant one less threat to Vicky.

And he would have continued his bait-and-destroy mission for as long as it took—or he lived—until he happened across a certain news article.

Ripping it to shreds didn't provide enough venting satisfaction.

The roar he let out shook the walls of the room he rented by the day.

No holding back his anger. Not after seeing this.

They're dangling Vicky like a fucking carrot!

Completely, utterly, fucking unacceptable. He'd specifically asked Brody to keep his Pima safe, not put out an ad announcing her location. Might as well put a giant bull's-eye on her for every asshat with a fantasy of becoming a killer for hire.

And what of the coma claim? Gene didn't believe it, assumed it was part of a ruse comprised by Brody or Reid, but what if it wasn't? What did he truly know of what happened to Vicky once they parted ways? Had Brody gotten attacked before reaching Kodiak Point? *Is she injured in a hospital, alone and defenseless?*

Gene berated himself for not seeing them safely there. In his defense, he'd feared changing his mind during the journey. But now he wished he had.

The not knowing how she fared, if she truly was injured, gnawed at him.

I'll just go and have a peek. Or he could call and get an update from Brody.

No. Because that would signal his interest. Better he visit in person and not let anyone know he was there. He'd slip in. Then out again.

Ha. As if that would happen. Gene had been looking for an excuse, any pretext really, to run to Vicky's side. And now that he had one, he didn't hesitate.

True to his nickname, Gene ghosted into town under the cover of darkness, right past their sentries—if he'd not wanted to keep his presence a secret, he would have done something to make a mockery of their feeble defenses. Unnoticed— because he was just that good—he made it to the medical center where Vicky supposedly lay in a coma. He watched people coming and going. Noted the position of the cameras, easy enough to avoid under the cover of a shift change as their electronic eyes swiveled in the opposite direction.

Tiptoeing along in stocking feet—because, contrary to the movies, boots were never quiet on hard-tiled floors—he avoided the numerous monitoring devices on his way to the section they kept convalescing patients in. He waited for the nurse to leave her station on her rounds then ducked behind the counter out of sight to peruse patient records.

There Vicky was, in black and white, a whole clipboard of info about her situation, signed by the doctor. He noted her room number and headed there next, but he didn't need to enter her room to know Vicky wasn't in it. While he could smell faint traces of her, the fresher trail—which drove his inner bear crazy, with the outer man not far behind—led him to the opposite end of the facility to an unmarked door. A locked door behind which he knew with every fiber of his being was his Pima.

He didn't knock or let her know he was there. Nor did he lay his cheek on the barrier like those idiots did in sappy movies.

But neither did he entirely leave.

Exiting the building, he found some shadows to hide in. He kept watch. Watched as Reid, with his distinctive swagger, arrived and then escorted two bundled figures to his truck. Instead of trailing them, Gene cut across town to arrive at Reid's house, where he watched from the woods. The drapes over the windows were drawn, a precaution against prying eyes, but Gene knew Vicky was inside.

And so long as she was, he watched. He followed. He stood sentinel some more.

However, he didn't remain unnoticed. His chilly perch on the rooftop across from the medical building, while rife with hiding places, couldn't hide him from a certain wolf tracker.

Gene didn't bother moving or greeting Brody when he settled in beside him the next day.

"I wondered how long it would take before you showed up," stated Brody.

It should have bothered Gene that his old friend guessed his baiting action would draw Gene to Kodiak Point. However, the well of anger that had fueled him for so long seemed to have run dry, dry where they were concerned at least. Hurt his Pima, though, and he would easily erupt. "I should kill you for using her as bait."

"Oh please, you and I both know it's our best chance at catching this guy. Or girl. Or whoever it is you think is targeting her."

"Maybe. But it's risky."

"Name a plan that isn't. According to reports, your girl disappeared into thin air from the expedition she was on. Authorities thought she was dead. We had to do something to draw the killer's attention."

"By having her at the very hospital you're trying to lure the assassins to?"

"She insisted on helping keep watch."

Gene snorted. "My Pima, insisting?" Surely he misheard.

"Your little lady can be quite stubborn."

Again, Gene couldn't help his incredulous tone. "Are we talking about the same woman here? Short, curvy, and wearing those stupidly hot glasses?"

Laughter erupted from Brody. "Yes, I'm sure. Seems her association with a certain crass bear has resulted in her growing a spine. Next thing you'll know, she'll turn out as bossy as Tammy or Jan."

Wouldn't he love to see it? Too bad he wouldn't. "I guess now that I know this whole coma thing is part of your plan I should leave."

"And miss all the fun?" Brody snorted. "Please. You and I both know this is where you want to be. Actually, I'll wager down there with that little human is what you really want."

Yeah, but he wouldn't give in to temptation. "My being here is putting you all in danger."

"I'd say having you on our side gives us an advantage."

"How do you figure that?" Gene asked, averting his gaze for a moment from the building to eye Brody.

"First off, you made it past our ring of sentries unnoticed. We could use your skills to beef things up around here."

"Me a teacher?"

"You could channel your inner sarge."

The idea did have some appeal. *The things I could teach those young pups and cubs that I learned in the military.* Still though, putting down roots? "I'm a magnet for trouble."

"And? Nothing wrong with a little excitement to keep a clan strong. Complacency kills. As does a stubborn refusal to accept a helping hand. Or paw. How many times do I have to tell you we're stronger together? I know you were probably dropped on your giant squash of a head a few times as a child, but still, even you're bright enough to understand the concept behind strength in numbers."

"I also know the benefits to ripping out the tongues of people who annoy me," Gene growled.

"I can feel the love. How I've missed your gentle camaraderie."

"Gentle?" Gene made a disparaging sound. "I see our experience didn't destroy your fucked sense of humor."

"Sometimes laughter is all we have." Brody's mien turned serious. "We all emerged scarred from our experience, Ghost. But some of us choose to not let it dictate our future."

A part of him wanted to scoff. Instead, he found himself asking, "How?"

"By allowing ourselves to live. By caring for others."

"But caring hurts." And admitting it aloud made him squirm, so he scratched a manly part to ensure his balls were still intact.

"Funny, because I'd say your plan to not care is hurting you even more."

Stupid jerk pointing out the obvious. "I hate you."

"Because I speak the truth. How long are you going to run from the fact you love that woman down there? How long are you both going to suffer?"

He latched onto one word. "Pima is suffering?"

"Yeah, for some strange reason, the girl misses you. One would even say she's depressed."

"Not because of me." He couldn't fathom that.

"Like I said, strange. It seems, despite the fact you're an A-hole, the girl is fond of you. If you ask me, I think she was dropped on her head a time or two as well. How else to explain the fact that whenever you're mentioned she jumps to your defense like a rabid wolf protecting a pup?"

"She does?" The news spread warmth through him.

"Yup. You'd have been so proud when she stood toe-to-toe with Boris, without fainting I might add, to expound upon your heroic qualities."

Gene groaned. "She didn't."

"Oh, she did. Quite vehemently."

Emotions twisted inside him as he found himself torn between wanting to shake her for her erroneous belief he was heroic and the urge to kiss her senseless for thinking he was. How he missed her. These fleeting glimpses didn't help. They only made his craving worse and to hear she missed him too and came to the defense of his tarnished honor?

Is it any wonder I love her?

What. The. Fuck.

How had he gone from needing and caring to love? When?

Fuck. *I love her.*

Now that the L word had exploded forth, even if only in his mind, it remained, a resonating realization he couldn't shove back in a box, or bury in an unmarked grave.

While stunning, the knowledge didn't send him rushing to her side. He still wasn't convinced their being together was in her best interest. But it also cemented his reason for staying, and screw it if his presence drew the wrong kind of attention. If Reid and Brody didn't give a fuck, then neither would he, and should the worst happen, he'd do his best to fight. Kill. And protect.

Given his cover was blown, Gene accepted Brody's offer to use his place as a rest stop. Having a place to stash his shit was handy, as was the use of a shower and a bed to rest. But only when he knew Vicky was well guarded, which usually meant Brody switching spots with him and keeping an eye on her.

They fell into a routine of cooperation and renewed their old friendship with an ease that Gene never expected—yet enjoyed.

Accepting a small measure of aid didn't mean he eased up on his vigilance. Good thing too, because someone took the bait.

As spring turned to summer, pesky tourists made their way to this remote Alaskan town. Strangers, human and not, arrived, flooding the population with their strange scents, spending their tourist dollars. It was a nightmare to track all the new arrivals, yet there was no real way of stopping them. Not without drawing attention.

The influx provided the perfect cover for someone with nefarious intentions.

A new set of hired killers finally arrived, appearing inconspicuous in their regular clothes and entering the medical center, not as a group but individually and at intervals so they didn't call attention to themselves. Unlike in the movies, they didn't sport villainous sneers or skulk inside, gun in hand. Just regular Joes going to see the doctor. One even held a bloody towel over his hand.

Great cover.

Just not good enough. Gene's bear took notice and rumbled a mental warning. Yet Gene had already marked them the moment his gut said these were the guys they'd been waiting for.

As Gene jogged down the two flights of stairs to ground level, he dialed Brody, who, wearing an earpiece as he was currently playing the dummy, didn't reply but listened as Gene simply said, "It's time."

He hung up and tapped a text to Boris. *Move your moose ass.*

Before he put his phone away, there was one more person he needed to contact, the woman he owed a big apology to for turning her into a shifter, even if it turned out Gene had done Reid a huge favor. Still, there was no card that could properly convey *Hey, sorry for causing you some kickass fucking pain and making you turn hairy and grow big teeth.*

While at his watch post, Gene noted as Tammy left the place, to grab some food at the diner. Not wanting her to come back and walk into a possible gunfight, he messaged: *Not safe. Stay where u r. G.*

Screw waiting for a reply. He slid his phone in his pocket and fell into a jog as he made a beeline for the medical building. Entering it, he could hear the sounds of a fight, and he sprinted down the hall toward the commotion, but he skidded to a halt outside the door with the Brody patient decoy, for more than one reason.

First off, Brody already had things well in hand. His buddy—who didn't save any thugs for Gene to slap around—already had three of them down and groaning. As for the fourth, he didn't stand a chance against the wolf.

But that wasn't the only reason Gene paused. These weren't the hired killers he'd expected. For one thing, they were shifters. For another, he recognized one of them, the only one still standing. "You work for *him*," he growled.

Brody, who'd grabbed the fellow in a chokehold, held him aloft and turned his head. "Are you sure?"

"Very."

A feral smile split Brody's lips. "Awesome. Reid will definitely want to talk to them."

Reid could try, but Gene doubted he'd learn much. Without a name or a face, just fuzzy impressions and a strong need to obey orders, these minions to the puppet master wouldn't have much to tell. They never did. Which was why Gene was having such a hard time tracing a path back to the source of the attacks.

Speaking of which… He glanced at the camera in the corner of the room. What were the chances Vicky hadn't seen him?

A cowardly part of him wanted to slink away instead of dealing with her. But the bear slapped it down, stomped on it, and then sat on his yellow streak for good measure. Time to face the woman he couldn't stop thinking about.

The woman he could no longer avoid.

And didn't want to.

As he walked the hallway, which twisted and turned, the various additions to the medical facility over the years having given it an irritating layout, he couldn't help but rehearse what he'd say.

I'm sorry.

Sorry for running out without a word.

How have you been doing?

Had she missed him as much as he missed her?

I love you.

Because he did, despite the fact that caring for her exposed his weakness. A weakness his enemies knew about and weren't afraid to exploit.

The fact was, danger revolved around Vicky whether he was around or not. Maybe more, because at least if she was at his side, he would stop at nothing to keep her safe.

A belief reinforced by a cry of pain that he recognized at once as belonging to her.

Someone dares hurt her! Yeah, that wiped all thoughts from his mind but one.

Kill!

As Gene rounded the last corner, he skidded to a halt and eased silently to the open door. He halted at the edge and peered around the frame, a silent presence that knew better than to rush in. Startling a killer led to hostages getting killed. Since he wanted Vicky alive, taking stock of the situation, despite his urge to barrel in, took precedence.

The sight of Vicky on the floor, a purple bruise rising on the edge of her jaw, made him burn with anger but not as much as the realization of who stood over her, threatening. While Gene had let Vicky go in a physical sense, he'd not completely let go. He'd spent more time than a grown man should, researching her online. Learning everything he could which in this day and age, was more than people realized. He'd come across many pictures, especially in the news, of the car crash that took her husband— a puny fellow he could have taken out with one punch.

A puny fellow who currently stood over his woman, daring to threaten her.

It seemed a certain dead husband wasn't so dead after all. And there was the missing piece of the puzzle. How easily he could snap that scrawny fucker's neck—and enjoy it. However, he paused as Vicky questioned the asshole. Now that he was here, his Pima was safe. Let her find closure and answers. Besides, he was curious to see this new braver Pima he kept hearing about. He couldn't help the pride that surged in him at she bravely sputtered, "You rotten jerk."

Not the most vehement of verbal attacks but a good start. He could always teach her better words later.

"Not happy to see me, wife?"

"I thought you were dead."

"Surprise! Going to give me a hello kiss?"

Over my dead body.

Over hers, too, given the moue of distaste twisting her lips. "Like heck. I preferred you when I thought you were six feet underground. Why, Rick? Why and how did you fake your death?"

"Oh so many reasons, but the main one was for money. I spent years fudging the books at my company. Shifting funds and building a nest egg. The plan was to fake my death and start over somewhere tropical where a man with a few million could live like a king."

"Well, you obviously got away with making everyone think you were dead. Why come after me, because it was you, wasn't it? All those accidents and then those men on the arctic expedition."

"Yes, it was me. Dying and taking on a new identity was easy. Problem was someone must have gotten wind of my money maneuvers. All the funds I'd squirreled away got transferred, leaving me penniless. Until I remembered my rich wife."

"So you decided to kill me? That makes no sense. You were declared dead. They found a body in your car."

"A body that they assumed was mine."

"So you faked it. You're still dead in the eyes of the law. I don't understand how you thought you could hope to inherit my money if I died."

"A miraculous recovery of course. The beauty of a body burnt beyond recognition is that it can be anyone. In this case, I was mugged, a victim of a crime. My car stolen, my identity hidden from me because of a blow to my head, which caused temporary amnesia. Until I caught sight of a news article about the demise of a certain woman that would trigger my memories. Albeit too late. I'd return to life, a sad widower and sole heir of millions."

Millions? Biting his tongue was all that prevented Gene from making a sound. His sweet Pima was an heiress? He could have smacked his head against the wall. When she'd thrown forth the idea someone was after her money, he'd assumed she had a few hundred thousand from a life insurance payout. But millions?

The gap he'd thought love could span suddenly widened.

"So now what are you planning? Going to just kill me in cold blood?"

How brave she sounded. And alert. Pride swelled within him. She'd come a long way from the girl who fainted every time something shocking came her way.

"Well, I can't very well let you live," Rick said in a matter-of-fact tone, advancing on her.

"Especially now, since our little talk." From his pocket, he pulled a gun.

"What I don't understand is how you knew I was in this room and not in the bed?" she said, indicating the screens.

"I didn't, until I happened to be in the diner the other day when a woman came in and ordered a burger. A burger with a familiar set of toppings."

"Me and my craving for jalapenos, bacon, cheddar and mayo," she grumbled.

"You and your disgusting penchant for food proved your downfall because I followed your friend back and then saw her leave hours later with a friend. It wasn't hard to guess you weren't in that bed. How clever of you to set a trap. But not as clever as me." He waggled his weapon at her. "Enough blabber. Your friend will be back soon, and I'd prefer to not have to kill two of you."

"You won't get away with this."

"And who's going to stop me?"

Gene almost said *I will*, but Vicky said it first as she staggered to her feet. "I will."

"Has my fat nerd of a wife finally gotten a backbone?" Rick laughed with clear derision. "Too late." He aimed his gun.

Gene had heard enough. Yet, before he could step in and save Pima, she saved herself.

"No. If there's one thing I've learned since you died is that it's never too late to fix a mistake." She then lifted her arm and, without wavering, or hesitation, fired the weapon in her hand.

She was armed?

Damn, he almost wiped a tear in pride.

As Rick toppled over, the close target making it impossible for her to miss, she finally caught sight of Gene. The gun fell from her hand with a clatter, and she whispered his name before her eyes rolled back in her head and she crumpled.

She never hit the floor, not with Gene to catch her.

As he held her cradled in his arms, he brushed the hair from her face tenderly. "Oh, Vicky, my brave girl." He brushed his lips against hers. "What am I going to do with you?"

"Not run away, not this time," she murmured against his mouth.

Surprised, he drew back to find her staring at him. "You faked fainting again," he accused.

"Not quite. Although it was pretty damned close. But I couldn't let it happen. Not when I knew you'd be gone again once I woke up."

"For your—"

"Own good. Yeah. Yeah. I know the refrain. But you know what? I don't accept it."

"Excuse me?"

"No I won't," she said struggling to free herself from his arms. She stood and faced him, a brave little thing with flashing eyes behind huge lenses and hands planted on her hips. A feisty Pima who screamed sexy. "You are not running this time, Gene. I won't let you."

"Like you could stop me."

"Physically no, but I intend to try, and I will succeed."

A smirk curled his lips. "Really? And how do you intend to accomplish that? I don't see an army. Or handcuffs."

"I won't need them."

"Then you can't stop me. This is for the best." Before he'd entered the room, he'd convinced himself they could make it work, but knowing his Pima was wealthy, and seeing her bravery, he got cold paws. *What can I offer her that she can't get herself?*

Much as it hurt, he'd turned to walk away when she said the one thing guaranteed to hit him hardest and destroy his chance at escape.

"I love you, Gene."
Damn.

Chapter Twenty-seven

Most women would have been crushed to see the effect the words I love you had on the man they declared them to. The slumping of his shoulders. The heavy sigh. The lowly uttered, "Why did you have to do that?"

"I said it because it's true. I love you, Gene, and nothing you do or say will change that. You can walk away now. Run if you want, but that won't stop me from looking for you."

"Looking for me will draw attention."

"Probably. But I don't care. Life without you sucks. It's lonely, and boring, and quite honestly, I don't want it. I don't care how safe it is. I'd rather live on the run or in a shack with you than without you."

He didn't say anything for a moment, and she held her breath, her moment of bravery fading the longer he went without answering. Had she misjudged? She'd thought for sure when she saw him standing there that it could mean only one thing. *He loves me.* Why else would he have shown up unless he was watching over her?

A man who didn't care wouldn't have bothered. Or so she hoped.

She almost missed his reply he spoke so low. "I have nothing to offer you. No riches. No house. Not even the promise of safety."

"I'm not asking for those things. All I want is you."

She squeaked as his arms came around her in a crushing hug.

"And I want you too, but—"

She hushed him with a kiss, a kiss into which she poured as much of her love and need as she could. To her relief, he returned it plus some, along with tongue action which turned her legs to rubber. She didn't fall though, not with Gene holding her.

When they finally came up for air, he growled. "Since when do you play dirty?"

"Since a certain bear taught me that being timid and nice won't get me anywhere."

"Staying with me is consigning yourself to a life on the run."

"Or not," interjected Reid as he entered the room and interrupted the moment.

Gene sighed. "I swear, Pima, you're worse for me than silver. You addle my wits."

Which, while he meant as a complaint, she took as a compliment. She doubted much frazzled her bear. To know she did warmed her from head to toe.

Reid laughed. "That's got to be a first. Me sneaking up on the infamous Ghost. Hello, Gene. Long time no see."

As Gene turned to face the alpha of Kodiak Point, he kept Vicky tucked into his side, where she felt the evidence of his tension in his rigid body. "Reid. I see you've recovered from our meeting."

"Never better. I trust you remember my mate?"

Tammy peeked around Reid's bulky form and grinned. She also winked at Vicky and mouthed, *Told you so*.

As in 'told you Gene cared'. There went the twenty dollars they'd wagered.

Gene actually fidgeted. "Is this where you shoot me for what I did to your woman?"

"Actually, I wanted to say thank you," Tammy replied. "Because of your generous blood donation I no longer need a frying pan to keep my bear in line."

"And as I keep telling you, it wasn't the cookware that made me fall for you but your damned mouth. Which I will gag if you don't behave."

"Behaving is overrated," sassed Tammy. "Just ask Vicky. I'll bet she'd agree. Bad girls have more fun."

"I don't know if I'd go so far as to call myself bad. But I'd definitely say that toeing the line does get dull." She noted Gene's surprised look and grinned.

"I'd like to know how this conversation got off track. I thought we were discussing convincing Gene to stay," Reid interjected.

"Oh, he's staying," Tammy stated with confidence. "Because it's his best shot at keeping Vicky safe."

"Not with the security you've got watching this place," Gene grumbled.

"Which is why we need you. I need you." Reid faced his old friend, and Vicky could not only see, but also feel, the tension running through Gene. "We need your expertise when it comes to setting proper perimeters. We need you to teach our younger clans members how to defend our clan and spot intruders."

Gene sighed. "Need. What is it with that damned word suddenly following me around? Since when did I become such a popular guy? Did I accidentally let my membership to Bad-Guys-R-Us expire?"

"The only thing bad about you is your attitude, but I've got a solution for that," Reid replied.

"Oh yeah. What?" mouthed Gene at his most belligerent.

The fist that hit Gene in the jaw might have snapped his head, but it barely budged his body. It also resulted in him…laughing?

Indeed, Gene chuckled. "Finally. A more manly response instead of all this touchy-feely shit. I'll stay, but only because you obviously need me. Your defenses suck. But I'll warn you like I warned Brody, no goddamned singing. Or barbecues. Or anything too fucking domestic. A man can only handle so much."

"We're not some fucking yuppie commune," Reid growled. "But we are clan, a clan that needs to talk apparently. But not today. It's late, and we've got cleanup to do before any of the tourists see something they shouldn't. Such as this guy. I take it you took care of him."

"Not me, but my Pima here," Gene said with obvious pride. "Say hello to the source of her attacks. It seems her ex-husband wasn't as dead as everyone thought."

"He certainly is now," Reid remarked, "which means no one will miss him when we make his body disappear."

"What of the other guys, the ones who went after the decoy?" Gene asked.

"All shifter. And the only one conscious isn't talking yet. We're going to put them on ice while we wipe any evidence."

"Need a hand?"

"Not for this. Besides, I think Vicky might be in need of a bit of companionship, as the shock seems to be setting in."

Indeed it was, a shiver making her shake as her gaze was snagged by the body on the floor. *Rick.* A man, who even dead, had tried to hurt her.

Not anymore. For the first time since she'd begun her abusive relationship with Rick, she'd stood up to him. She'd not allowed him to perpetrate his cycle of violence on her. *I don't have to take abuse, from anyone.*

Of course, she probably wouldn't necessarily resort to such permanent methods with everyone, but in this case, given his attempts to murder, she felt justified. She could console herself with the knowledge that, if she hadn't, Gene would have. She'd seen the murderous look in his eye on the monitors when he entered the decoy room. He'd been ready to tear apart those he thought attacked her.

So hot.

Almost as hot as the arm he slung around her, which hugged her against his solid body. She tuned back in to the conversation.

"I want you to take Vicky back to my place. Tammy will be along shortly. I've already got men positioned around it."

"Then what?"

"Then you meet back with me and we question the sneaky bastards who went after your woman."

The shudder that went through Vicky this time had little to do with the fact she'd killed someone and more because of the deadly tone Gene used when he said, "Oh, they'll be answering for that. Loudly."

The men shared a dark chuckle.

"Torture the bad guys, get some intel, and then," Tammy said brightly, interrupting the deadly intensity. "Rinse off the blood, grab a few cases of beer, and meet back at the house. I think it's time all you boys got together for a barbecue and, over copious amounts of roasted meat and booze, finally stop hiding from what happened and hash it out."

"Does she know what she's suggesting? The shit that could happen?"

A forbearing expression creased Reid's features. "Yes. She knows."

"She's nuts," Gene muttered.

"But mine," Reid replied fondly as he hugged Tammy to his side. "Enough blabber. Get out before I change my mind and have you work all night instead."

"Fuck that, Pima and I need to *make up* for lost time."

The unexpected innuendo brought heat to her cheeks that didn't cool until they hit the cold air outside. The coat she hastily threw on wasn't zippered and Gene brushed her trembling hands aside to take care of it. She pulled her gloves from her pocket along with her hat, stalling gestures because she didn't trust herself to speak. Thankfully, he didn't require words.

To her surprise, he laced his fingers through hers as they walked. It was oddly touching.

She recognized the truck he led her to as Brody's. "Won't he be mad you're taking it?" she queried as he helped her in, his large hands easily grasping her around the waist and placing her on the passenger seat.

"Brody knows I have the keys. I've been staying with him."

That jerk. And he'd never once breathed a word to Vicky despite seeing her daily. "How long have you been there?"

"Long enough," Gene replied as he put the truck into gear and pulled away from the curb.

She had to ask. "Why?"

"Because I couldn't stay away from you. Because I had to make sure you were safe." He paused, and she thought he was done. "Because I love you."

The dizziness had little to do with fear this time but more with exhilaration as he'd finally said aloud the words she'd longed to hear.

"I love you, too, Gene. Bear, killer, and all."

The truck swerved before she'd even finished talking as he pulled it over and rolled to a stop in the empty parking lot of a store closed for the night.

Why on earth are we stopping? A question answered as he leaned over and kissed her.

And kissed her some more.

And then kissed her some more. Despite their public location, Vicky couldn't help but fall under his sensual spell. He touched her, and her body responded instantly. His tongue probed the seam of her mouth, and she opened it, encouraging a wet tongue duel.

Making out in the front seat of a truck, in a parking lot. How crazy. Insane. Utterly exciting. Old, shy Vicky might have shied from it, but the new her, the more daring version, found it enflamed her. To know Gene wanted her so badly he couldn't wait, was there any better compliment?

A cry escaped her as his fingers tugged at the waistband to her pants. Gone were the thick layers required for warmth. It made his exploration easier. Vicky closed her eyes, anticipation tickling her. His hand cupped her mound inside her slacks, a sex hot and ready, covered only by a thin layer of cotton.

With maddening slow strokes, he rubbed her through the fabric, circular motions designed to have her trembling. If he kept at it, she wouldn't last long, not with the tension already coiling within her. In need of distraction, she groped at him, her hand landing on his corded thigh encased in athletic pants. She skimmed his firm upper leg until she reached a prominent bulge, and then she rubbed.

Oh, how he groaned. "Vicky."

It seemed her touching had a stimulating effect, as with a growl against her lips of, "Mine," he tore at her panties, the ripping fabric loud in the truck, even over their matching panting breaths.

His lips caught her blissful cry as he inserted two fingers into her sex while his thumb rubbed at her swollen clit. She couldn't help but grip him tight, and he gasped.

"Sorry," she apologized, releasing him.

"Don't stop," he rebuked, placing her hand back atop his erection.

Fascinated that he enjoyed something so simple as her rubbing him, she squeezed, only to gasp as he worked her faster. His fingers slipped in and out of her quivering sex while the friction of his thumb on her clit coiled her arousal tighter and tighter.

Then peaked.

Her orgasm hit, and she buried her face in the curve of his shoulder, pressing her lips against his flesh as she shook in the throes of her climax. Only when the shudders in her sex subsided did he withdraw his hand whilst giving her tender kisses.

He started the truck, and Vicky realized he was about to leave before getting his just due. Not this time.

They said giving was a great way of thanking someone. No time like the present to test that theory.

Her fingers dug at the waistband of his pants.

"Vicky," he growled in soft warning. "What are you doing?"

"Returning the favor."

"You don't have to do that. Trust me when I say the pleasure was all mine."

"I'm not doing this because I think I have to. I'm going to admit a little selfishness and say I'm doing this for me."

"You?"

"I want to touch you."

Oh how his gaze smoldered at her words. It made her more determined than ever to return the pleasure.

"We really should go somewhere a little safer."

No such thing existed. And besides, wasn't it safe enough a moment ago when he once again brought her to ecstasy?

She ignored him and kept shoving at the fabric hiding her prize. She almost yelled "Aha" as his erection sprang into her waiting hands. The lack of lighting made it hard to see, but she could certainly feel him as she clasped his rod and stroked it.

A velvet-covered, long, and thick steel shaft. A good thing she already knew it fit, else she'd have worried, given its girth. As it was, gripping him with her fingers, she reveled in its rigid state. *I excite him.* A heady feeling for a girl still rebuilding her self-esteem.

Brushing her thumb over the tip of it, she found herself smoothing the drop pearling there. But she didn't just want to touch. She wanted to taste him as he'd tasted her. Wanted to see if, as in all other things, this kind of intimacy with Gene would prove pleasurable.

Adjusting her position in her seat, she leaned over and took him in her mouth. He instantly reacted, his hips bucking. She could have grinned at this evidence of the effect she had on him. Not losing her latch on him, she let go of his rod to brace her palms on his thighs. At his low groan, she grew bolder. She sucked him deep then deeper. Uncertain what to do, she let instinct guide her, and instinct said to clamp her lips tight and suction.

Given the rigidity of his body, he definitely enjoyed that. So she kept at it, adding a bit of slide to her intent suckling of his shaft. His fingers threaded her hair, cupping her as he panted. "Yes. Fuck yes."

She increased her pace and knew he'd reached his peak when his hips thrust forth and held, pushing him deep into her mouth. She almost pulled away, unsure of what to expect—she'd never had a man come in her mouth before—but it was too late. He creamed her, and she found herself swallowing and even licking him clean.

The most relaxed chuckle she'd heard from him yet shook his body as he drew her up, placing a light kiss on her mouth. "You are full of surprises, Pima."

Apparently. And she couldn't wait to explore them with him. Alas, it would have to wait another night. Once he'd ascertained she was safe at Reid's home, and with a toe-curling kiss, he left her, but not before she made him promise to return.

"Nothing can take me from you now," he vowed. And Vicky trusted he would return. Trusted his love.

Chapter Twenty-eight

Despite not wanting to leave Vicky, Gene knew he had to. Protective instinct meant solving the mystery of *him*.

With several of *his* men in custody, perhaps they'd glean a clue, anything to lead them back to this mysterious leader with the magical-seeming powers. Gene wouldn't hold his breath though. Despite his grounded nature, Gene had come to the conclusion something unusual was at play, some dark and evil magic that kept the guy's identity a secret.

But no one was perfect. They were due for a clue. Something. And when they found it, they'd crack that mystery. *Then we'll kill the threat.*

Gene met Reid at the company garage, a large hangar situated in a nonresidential area—which meant no one to hear the screaming. As if anyone would complain. Well tourists might, but there was no reason for them to venture this way. As for the clan? Shifters weren't disturbed by violence and when it came to clan safety, there were no courtesy rules. Hell, most of the inhabitants would hold a threat down while another pulled at its claws in an attempt to make them talk.

As Gene entered the lit garage, he could hear Reid shouting. "How the fuck did they all manage to kill themselves?"

Say what? Gene broke into a jog and came around a large semi-truck to see Reid pacing in front of a cage comprised of silver-coated bars, which contained three obvious corpses. The fourth had died at the hospital of a broken neck.

Scanning the bodies, Gene noted no signs of blood or trauma. So how had they died?

Brody crouched to the left of the portable prison and sniffed while Boris scowled. Another old member of their unit, Kyle, straddled a barrel, whittling at a piece of wood.

Just like the old fucking days.

"Poison?" Gene queried.

"Suicide capsules? Not common because it takes a heck of a poison to kill a shifter so quickly, but not unheard of," Brody replied as he got to his feet and brushed his dusty hands off on his jeans.

"Just who the fuck are we dealing with that he feels a need to equip his minions with bloody poison pills?" Reid demanded. "I'm getting tired of this bullshit. No one knows who this guy is. He throws men away like they're meaningless. He obviously wants something, but what? I mean, if he wants rulership of the clan, why not come out and challenge me? Why all these useless petty games?"

Why did he want to make Gene believe it was his old buddies' fault he was kept captive for so long? Yet another question, Gene silently added to the list. It frustrated him he had no answers. The only things he knew, that any of them truly knew, was the danger existed, vigilance was needed, and violence—fist pump—would happen.

Gene just wouldn't have to face it alone anymore.

He was now back with brothers. His family. And he now had a woman.

My woman. Mine.

When no answers were forthcoming, and with night fallen, they decided to reconvene the next day. As Gene left with Reid, having given Brody back the keys to his truck, silence stretched between them, not one stilted or uncomfortable but one that came from familiarity and trust. Each had their own demons and issues to deal with, but the one that existed between them was no longer there.

Gene was ready to let go of the past—and live for the future.

As they took the road to Reid's house, back to his Pima, Gene couldn't help but mull over recent events.

The tryst with Vicky in the truck earlier that eve surprised Gene on many levels. For one, he'd let down his guard and indulged in a totally spontaneous, pleasurable moment. He'd meant it only as a chance to ease his need for Vicky by bringing her to climax. He certainly never expected her to reciprocate and to enjoy it so much, especially since, in between groans of pleasure, he'd tried to keep an eye on their less-than-secure surroundings.

It seemed his Pima had blossomed, gaining confidence and, in an odd twist because of it, had decided she wouldn't let him go.

She loves me.

Loved him.

Mine.

There was something innately powerful about knowing someone in the world cared for you. It didn't completely erase his past. It wouldn't dispel the nightmares. Or rid his life of danger. But it did fill him with hope. Hope for a future, a chance at happiness.

I am a polar bared with all my faults and yet still accepted.

As they arrived at Reid's home, Gene ignored Reid's chuckle as he said, "Someone a little impatient?"

Damned straight he was. He took the stairs in pairs to find his Pima. When he entered the room, he thought she slept, but if she did, his arrival changed that. She woke and stretched with a smile.

"Hi." How happy she looked to see him.

And it wasn't just his cock that was happy to see her, but given the lack of blood to his brain, coherent thought pretty much escaped him, as did full sentences. "Less talk. More nakedness," he grunted as he tore at his clothes.

A primal need to claim her made him rush, thick fingers tearing at garments that refused to cooperate. *Why must my shirt work against me?*

She giggled. "Take your time. I'm not going anywhere."

No, she wasn't. That didn't ease his need. On the contrary, the reaffirmation that she'd chosen him made his cock thicken painfully.

Throwing back the sheets, he could have laughed when he saw her familiar flannel jammies. "From now on, there's only one bear I want to see you wearing in bed, and it's not these," he murmured before divesting her of it.

Nude, her glorious, rounded body proved too great a temptation, and he practically threw himself on her. She welcomed him with an embrace of her arms and lips.

He finally let her breathe while he took a moment to stare at her. What a sight she made with her bee-stung lips and eyes hooded with desire. And not an ounce of fear.

She looked at him, scars, scowls, and all, yet didn't cringe. Knew what he was capable of— death, violence, and more—but didn't run. She knew who he was, and still, she loved him.

Easing himself onto a propped arm, he took a moment to admire her. He ran a calloused finger down her body, from the dip at the base of her throat, where her pulse fluttered, through the valley between her large breasts with the lovely, fat nipples, and over the round softness of her belly to the neatly trimmed curls at the juncture of her thighs.

"Beautiful," he muttered. Beautiful and his. His for claiming.

He started with the rapid pulse at her throat, sucking at the tender skin and leaving a hickey behind when he slid his mouth down to her breast. While her plump nipple beckoned, he held off, instead twirling his tongue around the begging berry. She shuddered then shuddered again as he rubbed the edge of his jaw against the tip.

"Oh, Gene."

How he loved it when she sighed his name. Opening his mouth wide, he latched onto her bud, a hard suck and tug that had her arching her back and desperate fingers clasping his head.

Incoherent cries left her as he tortured first one breast then the other.

Her hips gyrated, a not-so-subtle invitation to sate her arousal. He ignored it. He had fantasized about this moment too many times to rush.

But he did offer her some comfort. As he licked and sucked at her gorgeous breasts, he slid his hand down between her thighs and cupped her.

Hot. Damp. Trembling.

She was so ready for him.

Between her slick folds, he dipped a finger, his cock jerking in response to the twitch of her channel. She wouldn't last much longer. She hovered on the edge. With a few strokes of his fingers, he could probably make her come, but this time, the selfless lover was gone.

The greedy man, the needy soldier, wanted to feel her climax around his cock. Bracing himself on both arms, he poised himself over her.

Her beautiful eyes opened, and the most wondrous smile curved her lips as she breathed, "Gene."

She looped her arms around his neck and drew him down for a kiss as he thrust into her. He caught her keening cry with his mouth, felt the tremble of her sex as it clung tight to his shaft.

He stroked in and out of her welcoming flesh, and she responded with a wanton abandonment that awed him. Enthralled him.

I do this to her. I bring her this joy.

Just like she brought joy to him. Faster he pumped. In and out, the tension coiling, the ecstasy building until it culminated in one shining moment.

Bliss.

Heaven.

Love.

Home.

Home at last, in the arms of a woman who loved him.

Epilogue

"Someone is going to die," Gene declared. He would do it himself, with his bare hands. Slowly. Torturously.

Vicky stuck her head around the bathroom doorjamb to ask, "Who? And why?"

"Someone who thinks they're fucking funny." Not. As to the why, he held the reason aloft.

Pushing her glasses into place, his Pima perused the offending item. Then she had the gall to snicker. "Is that a superhero outfit?"

"Yes," he replied through gritted teeth. It had arrived in an unmarked box on the front step, addressed to him.

At first, he'd feared a bomb, and after ensuring Vicky was tucked safely away where a blast wouldn't reach her, he'd tossed a few rocks at the package. When it didn't explode, he then placed his ear on it, listening for any ticking sounds. He'd smelled it too.

When nothing suspicious happened, he carefully took his knife to the tape holding it shut. Lifting the lid, he encountered a layer of tissue paper under which lay the atrocity.

He now wagged it like a flag in the air. Black leather pants with a big white G on the ass. Leather straps to crisscross his chest, again with the Giant G emblem on the front. And to top it off, a fucking spiked collar with, you guessed it, another G.

Someone with a warped sense of humor and too much time on his hands was asking for a maiming.

"Are you going to try it on?"

Surely his incredulous expression answered that dumb question.

Vicky giggled. "Oh come on, it's not that bad."

He held it aloft again. "Not that bad? It's a fucking fetish outfit on superhero crack."

"I think it's thoughtful."

"How do you figure that? I'm being mocked."

"I would have said commended for your heroic side."

"I'm not a hero," he growled. Except where she was concerned. For his Pima, he'd do anything. As for anyone else, they could kiss his ass—an ass without a giant G.

Okay, so he lied a little. He wouldn't just help his Pima. He might give a hand to his friends, no one else, and even then, only if he got to hit something— or scored free beer.

"You're my hero," she proclaimed before disappearing back in the bathroom to do who knew what. She shouldn't have bothered. Gene loved her as she was. Dressed in fuzzy pajamas with polar bears wearing red scarves. In long johns splayed across his snowmobile in the woods. Naked with her hair spilling over her shoulders and wearing those sexy glasses of hers.

Mmm. Hungry. Need. Her. Now.

Why is she taking so long? "What are you doing?"

From the bathroom, she didn't answer his question but instead said, "I, for one, would like to see you in the outfit."

"Like fuck."

"Not even if I was dressed as your sexy sidekick?" Vicky emerged from the bathroom, and Gene could only stare. He might have drooled a bit too.

He didn't dare blink, too afraid the sexy vision would disappear. *She is so damned beautiful.* White blouse tied off under her ribs, see-through to show off a black lace bra. A tight black mini skirt. High heels. Hair atop her head in a messy bun and, of course, sporting those hot dark-rimmed glasses. She looked every inch the naughty librarian until she turned around and showed him her butt. Across the skirt was another emblem, *G's*.

Mine. Oh yes. All mine.

And he was hers. A hero in her eyes, a villain in the eyes of others. Not that he cared. The only opinion that truly mattered was strutting toward him with a come-hither smile and a sexual confidence that excited him.

Who knew love would see his Pima blossom? Who knew the threat of danger would bring out the warrior in her?

How did I ever get so lucky to have the most wonderful woman in the world fall in love with me?

He counted his blessings every day, just like he thanked her every day, not just by making love to her luscious body. For her, he'd settled in to Kodiak Point. He accepted a role as head surveillance dude. He implemented as many warning systems as he could to protect the town—and his Pima. They bought a house. They became a part of the clan. A polar bear and his human.

A man and his woman.

For her and her alone, he dropped his plans for vengeance. A polar bear, and a man, laid bare in the face of her love, and accepted.

In spite of having escaped his prison a while ago, only now did he finally feel free. And happy.

*

'Twas the eve of the solstice and all through the town
Not a creature was stirring, not even to frown.
The shotguns were lined by the doorways with care,
Packed with silver shot, evil shifters beware.

The wild animals were tucked all snug in their dens
While visions of the hunt danced in their heads.
The alpha and his mate, all snug in their cave,
Had just adjourned but didn't plan to behave.

When out of the woods there arose such a clatter
The shifters all sprang to see what was the matter.
Out on the ridge, muzzle held high to the stars
Was a single wolf, howling warning from afar.

Stars twinkled, illuminating the ground below,
And dispelled the shadows that crept in real low.
With a roar of challenge, and a split of their skin,
The clan shifters arose to engage attacking kin.

A mighty battle was fought, not without casualty,
But a surprising hero arose out of the calamity.
A ghost, a savior, a bear of pure white,

Came roaring from his den to help them smite.

And when the attackers were rebuffed,
And sent on their way,
The victors all cheered,
With an ululating hooray.

As for the wolf,
Who'd given them fair warning,
He came across a prize,
And thought he was lucky.

But as he was ambushed and taken,
Not without a valiant fight,
He couldn't help but wonder
If he was in a dire plight.

Because the one who captured
Was not what she seemed,
And sometimes the true story
Remains to be seen.

To the woman who'd led to his ignoble capture,
Brody, the wolf, couldn't help but mutter.
"You may think you have me now,
but only for the moment,
In the end I shall escape
And cause you sensual torment."

The End

The series continues with Brody in Wolf's Capture or for a Kodiak Point, holiday treat, check out Caribou's Gift. More info at EveLanglais.com

Made in the USA
Lexington, KY
19 February 2019